THE BREAK

Deb Fitzpatrick lives and works in Fremantle, WA. She has a Master of Arts (Creative Writing) from the University of Western Australia and occasionally teaches professional writing and editing at Curtin University. Deb is the author of *The Amazing Spencer Gray* (2013), a novel for younger readers. Her novels for young adults – *90 Packets of Instant Noodles* (2010) and *Have You Seen Ally Queen?* (2011) – were both awarded Notable Books by the Children's Book Council of Australia. *The Break* is her first book for adult readers.

visit the author: debfitzpatrick.com.au

book club notes: fremantlepress.com.au/books/adultfiction

THE BREAK

DEB FITZPATRICK

for Mum and Dad

The water in our blood will be cloud one day.
And was glacier aeons ago.

from *The Drowner,* Robert Drewe

A great tree stands in the southern corner of Western Australia, its bark carved with lines like rivers. Marri: the Nyoongar word for blood. Corymbia calophylla*: given the common name marri because its sap is the colour of blood, oozing down woody bark into hard, jewelled sores.*

The broken old marri arm hides a narrow hollow. Tucked inside in a plastic bag is a rolled-up map of the night sky, protected from the wind and rain and sun. The great tree swings restless next to a wide weatherboard house, next to a dark and moving river, next to the blue fusion of two oceans. If you stood beneath that tree you would see it all: the house, the river, the blue-gum plantations, the forest rambling around and between. At night, you'd see the Southern Cross hanging like a child's kite in the sky. And, if you closed your eyes, you'd see further still: the road leading to Greys Bay, where the bush ends and the limestone coast reaches out, and where the horizon opens so wide it reveals the very curve of the earth.

1

They'd sent Rosie Curran to make a story out of a young man's despair, though not in so many words. A story, about a guy leaping from the Leighton Beach tower – a *story*, for a newspaper, for people to sit down with over their morning cuppa, their bowl of muesli, their day ahead.

She'd looked straight at Frank, the news editor who farmed out each day's stories to the staff, but he wasn't going to turn flexible all of a sudden, not Frank.

'A suicide story, Frank?' she said.

'A public interest story,' he corrected. 'The psych unit turned the kid away last week.'

Rosie tried to imagine herself actually going there, waiting on her favourite beach, waiting under the tower with a speck of a man at the top. It could have been anyone – someone she knew, a friend – Christ! Anyone. And this wasn't the first rubbish story she'd had to do for *The Messenger*, for her stupid career, for the advertising people upstairs.

She was over it. Rosie, aged twenty-two, couldn't believe she'd stuck it out this long.

'For Christ's sake, Frank...' She followed him into the kitchen, where the benchtop was a work of art, a collage of mug rings and shrivelled teabags. 'I don't want to go and watch a guy trying to do himself in.'

'Rosie,' he laughed, 'it's the nineties – nothing's sacred anymore.'

Isn't it? she thought. She took a breath. 'But this is a community newspaper! Surely there's another story I can cover, I mean, it's what we put in the paper that becomes news –'

'Rosie, it's a story, you're a reporter. Go and do it, alright?'

She went out to the car, took a few breaths under the jacaranda tree and weighed up her options. She could either do the story, pretend to do the story, or outright refuse to do the story.

Panic crawled out of its nasty place. She felt her temperature climb. Who was she kidding? This wasn't a school project, this was her fucking *job*. This was the rent, food in the fridge. Her future.

She looked west. The beach wasn't far away. Leighton was where she and Cray spent most summer Saturday mornings, the corduroy sound of sand beneath their feet, the sun grilling them from above. There was something about those times at Leighton, something that Rosie risked forgetting in between. She'd stop there on hot evenings after work, when the sky went gentle, slipping into the end of another day, and when people were breathing again, breathing their own life.

2

Cray watched the clear water against his skin. Leighton never disappointed, always offered something different, depending on how he felt, depending on the swell, the wind, the sun. This beach didn't have the darker, moving water of beaches down south, where you always had to watch the current, check your position against the towels that were like compass points on the beach, make sure you hadn't moved out too far, or too close to the rocks. It was almost safer on a board, Cray often thought, at least you had something to float on, to cling to if need be.

On the sand, a beachcomber with a metal detector hovered close to Cray's gear, and Cray trod water a little harder, a little higher, keeping his eye on him. Harmless old coot, he thought, nothing better to do but scour the leftovers of other people's lives. He sank down into the cool, eclipsing the old man, and poked his toes about for sand, for an idea of his depth.

It was his week off. Cray had come down from the mine on Friday night – he always took the late plane, didn't want to spend any longer out there than he had to, the nights at the mess spent drinking, smoking, swearing. The guys out there could *drink*, the older guys who'd been there for years and who were never gunna leave – no reason to, no wife, no family, just hard work, huge pay packets and truckloads of beer for company. Thirty-year-old Cray couldn't keep up with them, and didn't want to. Three beers and he was wandering back to the donga for the night. He had one to himself, thank god, he couldn't have hacked sharing a place with a snoring, farting, hungover grader operator. Besides, it wasn't a good thing to get too matey with the fellas; sacking non-performers was another heartening part of his job as a project engineer. As was rousing them after a night on the piss. Cray frequently had to drive from donga to donga at five-thirty in the morning, feeling fairly ordinary himself, to bang on doors, and had even had to shake a few blokes from their beds when the morning-after blur was too much. Rounding 'em up like cattle.

Aaah. It was another world out there. You had to laugh. You had to.

Rosie had said, before she'd fallen asleep, 'What do you dream about, Cray?'

Cray thought, *That depends if I'm here with you or there, in the desert.* He was lucky to get to sleep at all out there some nights, lay awake worrying about contractors and designs and deadlines. But he was here now, he was home. And so he dreamed about the things he could enjoy the next day.

'Beaches,' he'd told her. 'Swell.'

'Nice,' Rosie said sleepily.

The shock of the water on sticky skin. The shifting of sand and shells as peelers came through. Cray was so bloody glad he and Rosie lived by the coast, the ocean just a skin-lick away. He only wished he didn't have to leave it all the time. Settling and unsettling.

He'd asked Rosie to stop calling him when he was up at Leonora. It was better not to go through those phone calls, better just to look forward to his week off, to seeing her. And it was good, having a whole week off. He really relaxed then, going to the beach, swimming, fishing, heading to the fish pub with Rosie for a few beers and a seafood feast. But the four weeks on site, they were long weeks. And the anticipation of them was worse than actually being there. And Shitslinger. Jesus.

Cray ducked under the surface and swam along the bottom to shore, seeing if he could make it without having to come up for air. He burst up in the warm shallows.

A thin smear of cloud shaded the water. Cray scanned the carparks, lined up side by side, beach by particular beach: Leighton – the bodysurfers' beach; then the Dog Beach; followed by Cables – one of Perth's excuses for a surf spot; Cottesloe – flesh, curves, oil and bikinis; and Swanbourne, where grown men wanked in the dunes.

Cray dried off in the carpark, next to the Woody, trying not to expose himself while he pulled off his boardies from under a towel wrapped around his hips. He headed home to read the paper and loll about in the hammock, a small shell from one of the rockpools on the dash for Rosie.

He was still looking at the swell as he drove away, so he didn't see the young man climbing gingerly down the long narrow ladder of Leighton Tower, and a few people at the bottom looking upwards, looking tired.

3

Rosie was ready. She opened the door to *The Messenger* offices.

'*The Messenger*, please hold,' one of the secretaries was saying into her headset. 'Is Freddo down there, Rosie, do you know?'

'Freddo?'

'Oh, sorry,' she laughed, turning slightly red. She covered the microphone. 'Frank. *Freddo the frog*,' she whispered. 'Look-alikes.'

Rosie grinned. 'Uh, I dunno,' she said, holding up an uneaten sandwich in a paper bag. 'I've been out.'

She headed down the corridor, past the room of deadline-fearing typesetters making an impressive racket on their keyboards; past subeditors swinging to the phone every now and then to check the spelling of a local councillor's name; quickly past the desk of the eccentric editor in case he pulled her aside to pass on another story or two; past the overburdened and bored-shitless real estate writer, who had three or four thesauruses in front of her in an effort to find different words to describe kitchens in houses that were all the same; and ended up at Frank's desk.

He still used a typewriter, insisted on it, despite the typesetters' complaints. 'You've gotta move with the times, Frank,' they'd implore. 'It takes ages to re-key your stories.'

'Move with the times?' he snorted. 'I'm the only one around here doing that! And if advancement is what everyone wants, why did we just put Johnny Howard into the top job?'

Standard operating procedure: turn a conversation about outmoded office equipment into political commentary.

He patted his beloved machine and said, 'No way. This fella's more loyal than most people.' And he looked meaningfully at one of the reporters.

Another of Frank's pet topics: loyalty.

'Did any of you see that silly trumped-up cow on Channel Seven last night?' he said to no one in particular. 'We taught her everything she knows, that girl. As soon as she'd sucked us dry she was out the door.'

Now Rosie stood close to his desk, not really knowing what she was going to do.

'Have you got a minute?' she said.

'What did you get?' he said, nodding at her sandwich bag, standing up.

'Huh? Oh ... ham and salad. They're in some kind of a food coma in that joint. I'm going to ask for pitta bread with hummus and sprouts one day, just to see how they react.'

Some staff looked up from screens and notes as Rosie and Frank walked out to the courtyard where people had lunch and cigarettes.

Rosie concentrated on how she was going to start this, how this would end.

'So Rosie-bosie, how'd you go this morning?' Frank asked.

How do you think I went, Franky-wanky?

'Well ...' She took a breath. 'I didn't go.'

He tried to look as though he wasn't surprised, but Rosie had seen this look before, and she knew it well; he was pissed off.

She went in to defend herself before he could engage in his ceremonial Tearing Strips Off Stupid Young Reporter ritual. As if from a distance, she heard her voice thin with exasperation and her pitch rise, but, worse, she was regurgitating all sorts of naive clichés: 'News is for informing people about what's going on around them; it's not about satisfying morbid curiosities; it's not just about getting people to buy the paper.'

Frank looked at her with amusement.

Rosie wanted to slug him. There was a limit to how cynical you could be, surely?

'Rosie, I sent you on a job, and now we've lost a story – a good story.' He stared at her more seriously, voice searing. 'What are you – a reporter or just another bloody pipedreamer?'

Inside, phone calls had been hung up on, the radio turned down.

Rosie met Frank's eyes. 'It wasn't a good story. It was a shit story. And you're spot-on; I'm not really a reporter, if that's what it's all about.'

'For god's sake, Rosie! Don't you want to sink your teeth into something real out there? Our readers have *the right to know* what their local mental health service does when a kid goes there. One day it could be *their* kid. This is important stuff; it's uncomfortable, yes. But sometimes when there's a tragedy, following the trail of blood is what needs to happen. If comfortable's what you're looking for, go and talk to Sharyn in *Lifestyle* – isn't she doing a story on nail polish at the moment?' He paused to catch his breath, then said, 'The thing is ... you could be really good at this. If you'd just ...' He sighed.

Rosie stared at the ashtray. Did she hear him right? *Following the trail of blood?* She felt disgusted – but she could see Frank's reasoning too. Maybe she was just being pathetically naive?

He walked back into the office without her, letting the door slam shut.

Naive. She could live with that. Rosie still couldn't do it. She could live with that too.

4

The green Kingswood was parked outside the front of the house, frangipani poking over the bonnet. Rosie went in and dumped some old notes and her favourite thesaurus onto their bed.

Cray was sitting out the back in the shade with the paper, the blue teapot close at hand.

'Hello!' he said, confused, looking at his watchless wrist. 'What's the time?'

She kicked off her shoes and walked over the cool grass towards his patch of shade. 'One, or something.'

He reached out for a cuddle.

'How was your swim this morning?' she grinned, deferring.

'Ahhh, like Esperance water, like out of a bottle. And I had a forage in a couple of the rockpools further up in the reef.'

The water was Cray's obsession, and he'd shared it with her from the day they met. The whole coastal world had opened up to her through him: reef breaks, wind direction, headlands, currents. Before Cray, she'd felt the coast wasn't her territory. But Rosie was glad to be let in to this blue, buffeted place – to be really let in – and it was one of the things she loved most about him.

'You didn't go past the tower, did you?' asked Rosie.

'Leighton tower?'

She nodded.

'Yeah. Why?'

'Some guy was threatening to jump off it, apparently. Frank tried to get me to go down there. Talk about ambulance chasing! Arsehole.'

Cray grimaced. 'What were you meant to do when you got there? Shout up a few questions?'

Rosie looked around the back garden, slightly dazed. She noted with weird relief that their back patio needed sweeping. 'So I, um, quit. I ... left. Gave *The Messenger* the flick.'

She scrunched and unscrunched her toes, and reached for the teapot. 'So. I s'pose I'll give this a refill.'

'Well, hang on.' Cray grabbed her hand, trying to stop her for a minute.

She blinked into the reinvented day. 'Let me put the kettle on first.'

Cray watched Rosie walk towards the kitchen, holding the pot loose-wristedly; it might have dropped and smashed if she'd loosened her grip on it any further.

She *quit*.

He was stunned, impressed. He knew she'd not loved being at the paper, but she'd always justified it as a stepping-stone, a way in. If only he'd had that kind of backbone when he was in his early twenties.

Cray watched a honeyeater plop into their birdbath and preen itself on the side of the terracotta bowl. When it had flown off, he filled up the watering can, crackled across the leaves and topped it up till the water's skin gripped at the edge. *Money,* he thought. *Bloody money. The stuff that gets you bread and milk and the latest LandCruiser is driving the world fucking bonkers – no one knows what they're doing anymore, just do whatever it is for the money, accumulate the stuff like food in a bomb shelter, just because everyone else does the same. People can't seem to bear the old brick barbie with a hotplate anymore, they need a top-of-the-range 'outdoor kitchen'. And a three-car garage that's nearly as big as their whole house. Justifying your crappy life by surrounding yourself with things provided by the money which is provided by the shit job that you absolutely hate. It was diagnosable, apparently: 'affluenza'.*

He nodded at the honeyeater, now in the fig tree, cocking its head at the shimmering water, and looked at Rosie through the kitchen window with pride.

Countless rockpools along that coast cup the small lives of anemones and barnacles. Strewn about in the rushing water, they come to rest on a jut of reef, bracing against the sudden cold barrages of the sea.

A hand plunges in. Resting on the pool bottom are broken pieces of shell, long vacated. The fingers sieve them like jewels, tiny flecks of the day, skin and sweat and the skin of others swirling perfectly into the solution.

5

Liza watched Sam run outside. He flailed his arms and yelled at a ginger cat that was pelting away, ears flat, towards a tree. It scaled the small gum looking back at the boy only when it reached the upper branches. Sam stared at it keenly.

Take that, cat, Liza thought. *You met the wrong Crowe today.*

Sam ran back inside, where Liza was slapping vegemite on thick slabs of wholemeal.

'Gotta keep that cat *away*, Mum – they eat native birds, you know.'

Liza sighed. Sam kept everyone on their toes, even the local felines. 'I haven't seen that cat ever catch a bird, Sam, and until I do, it's welcome in this house.' *Besides, it's good company,* she thought. It must have been Mrs Perry's; everywhere else was too far away from the farmhouse. It was always coming in through the back door – paw hooked around the flyscreen – and, well, what harm could come from giving the friendly creature a drop of milk every now and then?

'Now eat this.' She passed Sam a plate with two bits of bread on it. 'And no more snacks until your tea, okay?'

He looked pleadingly at her and said, 'But the fairy wrens! I saw that cat stalking one on the weekend!'

'Do you have any homework to do?'

'Yessss. Practise my spelling words. And do my reading. But can I go on the Mac for just a little while, Mum?'

She looked at her watch, then nodded. 'Half an hour, and then do your homework, okay, Sam?'

As he trotted down the corridor to his bedroom, she heard a faint *Okay, Mum* drift her way.

'Naaaaa!' Sam mimicked his Mac's 'on' sound as it booted up. He loved his computer, it was like having a secret companion in your bedroom – always there, waiting to start up, and a million different things to do on it. It was an old one, an LC 575, but he was hassling his folks for a 5400 for Christmas. Or maybe Christmas and birthday, seeing they were pretty expensive.

A year ago, when his uncle Mike last visited, he'd brought Sam a modem and had set him up with a dial-up account. Sam's dad had chucked a mega wobbly about it. He'd had a huge argument with Mike and raved on at him about *bloody asking one of us before you go and bloody do something like introducing a world of bloody rubbish to the kid.* Sam listened to the whole thing from his room, praying that he'd just get to keep the modem, which he did, but only after Mum had sorted the two of them out. She'd yelled, too, at both of them. She was the best. But she was strict about The Rules. Sam always had to ask if he could go online, and he was only allowed half an hour at a time. Except on weekends, when he sometimes got an hour.

So ever since then, Sam had been checking out some of the cool sites on the internet – and there were heaps. He clicked on one of his favourite sites, a sci-fi story, updated every day by some guy in the States.

The story just got better and better. He read it each day when he got home from school, after afternoon tea. It was mostly words, just a few pictures. He'd ask Mum, then run down to his room, which was pretty big, heaps of space for his star charts and models, and would power up his computer.

He knew Mum got cranky sometimes when he was on the net, but that was only when she was expecting someone to call and they couldn't get through because the modem was connected. Or when she was bored, waiting for Dad to come back from the trees. But Sam also knew that no matter how long he was on the internet, he'd *always* get one of Mum's hugs before bed. The other night she'd nearly squashed him into a cardboard cutout kid.

'Will we still do this when I'm, like, *twenty*, Mum? Do the superbearhug thing?'

She'd nodded surely. 'Yep, we will.'

Nine-year-old Sam already felt squirmy at the thought, embarrassed, but kind of glad, too. He couldn't imagine being twenty. He reckoned he didn't have to worry for a while yet. It was a long way away.

Sam concentrated now as his eyes scanned the screen. Valstran was getting closer – it wouldn't be long until he took over Sawan country. Jeez, if only he had that 5400 and Netscape, he'd have faster download speed and better graphics, too. Maybe he could talk to Mike about it. Yeah, he'd mention it to Mike next time he was down, whenever that would be.

6

Ferg wandered through the tiny orchard, his hand lingering on the trunk of a knobbled, grey-brown plum tree as he passed. The late afternoon sun filtered through the leaves of orange trees, avocados, lemons, an almond and a pear. There was a hedge of blackberries, a tangle of raspberries. A grand old fig. All this old stuff. He couldn't imagine his father planting it all, back in those early days. Trees need that, he thought. Long-term vision. You think you can't be bothered with the waiting, the *years,* but the things always grow, and transform the place with them. And it wasn't even business for his old man – Jack still had the dairy farm to look after, to keep turning over, day in, day out.

The orchard had been for Ferg's mum, for Pip. She was battling with the boys and was hopelessly homesick, she once told him. When they first built the house, it was full of fleas, didn't even have a proper floor, and she was pregnant. 'That's why your dad planted that orchard, to make things a little better for us.'

Ferg wished his old man were still around, would've loved to have a beer with him, hear more about those early years, see his mum with those grinning, shining eyes again. He knew that he and Sam and Liza weren't always such good company for her. He wondered if Pip looked at him and Liza, at how things were between them.

A few dry white skeletons in paddocks reminded him of how his father's generation had cleared the land, hacking away a ring of bark from the trunks, waiting for the things to die. Trees used to be their enemies, his dad had said when Ferg told him about the tree-farm idea. They'd only got in the way of farming the land. 'Good on you, son,' Jack had said from the couch. 'You're taking this old place into the next century. That's the way it's gotta be.'

Dairy farming wasn't the staple of this town anymore, not since the arrival of the alternative lifestylers in the seventies and the vineyards and now the tourists. Things had changed for the farmers around Margaret River; they'd had to change. Ferg grew Tasmanian blue gums on the property now, but he kept a small stock of milking cows, and the orchard, to remind him of how it all began. There was big money to be had from the blue gums, and while Ferg and Liza had only begun the business a few years ago, things were looking pretty good. It had been a worry when they'd taken the plunge, and the bank was worried too, but they'd done their research, and Ferg'd completed a few units in environmental science out at the ag college, where he'd been the oldest student by a couple of decades.

As for his brother – well, Mike had pissed off to the city.

Ferg took out the thermos of coffee he'd made that morning, realising as he swirled it around that he hadn't put any sugar in it. He swallowed the creamy stuff, trying not to taste the bitterness of it on his tongue.

7

Sam was busy charting constellations, lying on his belly on the rug, cold slits of draught coming up between the boards underneath. He heard the wind and the huge old marri going nuts out there, and was that someone knocking at the front door, or just his imagination *going wild*, as Nanna Pip would say? He imagined the wind was a superhero force, stealing the sound from the visitor, wrapping it up and sucking it down underneath the weatherboard house. (He'd explored under the house a couple of years ago, got his Darth Vader tracksuit pants all dusty, and found a cat's skull right under their fireplace. Mum didn't like the skull much, wouldn't touch it, but Sam heard her ask Dad later how long it might have been there. He'd strained to hear his father's reply, but couldn't move away from the window because he was keeping a log of shooting stars that passed over their house.)

The pale green paint was peeling off the outside of their place, but Sam liked it. The house was big and old and had heaps of different spots to explore. There was a fence where Mrs Perry's place began, it was bent right down where they climbed over it all the time, and it wasn't like other fences that you couldn't go over – like the one at school. Mrs Perry always said, 'Hello, Sam,' in that funny voice of hers when he was crossing through her garden to get to the hill, or the river. Mrs Perry was from Scotland, that's why she sounded funny. She called her chooks *chewks*. He loved the sound of their clucking and scratching and picking over the soil. Yep, he was glad they didn't live in one of the new houses in town. Little brick boxes, Dad called them, snorting. They were all the same – all *beige*, he said, with *beige* garage doors and *beige* carpet inside. Sam felt sorry for the kids who lived in those beige places, and sometimes brought home a friend, showed them his bedroom, with the big window, and the marri right next to the front door, and pointed to the purply-blue blur of the blue gums in the distance, where his dad was working. But he only showed the cat skull and his charts to Jarrad. He was the only one who understood that stuff. And he was into the internet.

The flyscreen door creaked like a bullfrog, and Sam heard the sound of Dad's voice, and another voice, but he couldn't hear well enough to tell who it was. The *wind*. It was really howling now, and Sam wondered if the marri would be okay – it was close to their powerline, and he got up real quick to ask Dad if any branches needed trimming, or anything. Sam didn't want to miss out on his sci-fi story, and besides, he didn't much like candlelight, which made everyone look spooky.

'Liza, Mike's been out on the verandah ...'

'Knocking away like an old dero.' Mike grinned stupidly.

Liza laughed. 'You dickhead, you should have just come in!'

'Dickhead!' he protested.

They were all laughing, standing in the kitchen.

Ferg wandered over to the kettle, shaking his head at the silliness. 'Who wants one?' he said, holding up his special after-work mug, a huge thing.

'Yeah, tea thanks, Fergs. But a normal mug'll do for me, thanks, mate.'

Liza tutted. 'Shame Pip's not here.'

'Where is she?' asked Mike.

Liza and Ferg looked at each other, then said in perfect timing, their voices a funny harmony, 'Ladies' bridge.'

'Ladies' bridge!' Mike smothered a laugh.

'She goes with Mrs Perry, once a fortnight.'

'No, sorry, that's good,' Mike said. 'It's good. Poor Mum. She must miss the old man like hell.' He shook his head.

Not that you do much about it, Ferg felt like saying. 'Reckon she does,' he said.

Fergus thought of their mother there, in the brightly lit hall with tables of oldies dealing cards. Pip wasn't really into bridge, he knew that. *I go for the social side*, she'd told him one day when they'd waited for Mrs Perry to bring the car around. Despite that, he reckoned it was a good thing. She usually came back pretty cheery, with a few bits of gossip about local goings-on.

Sam skidded in on his socks.

'Hey, Sam!'

Liza watched him take them all in before saying, 'Dad, do we need to check the marri, cos the wind's up and it might hit the powerline. Hi, Mike!'

They were all looking at Ferg, awaiting his response.

'Have you come to stay again, Mike?' Sam plopped down on one of the wobbly wooden chairs, remembering the time Mike stayed in the sleep-out a few years ago when Auntie Jenny went to Europe. Liza said Sam wasn't to bother him then, just let him be, when he had asked her why Mike looked sick, kind of bony, and never got out of bed until after lunch.

'No, no, mate, just come to say hi. I was on a job out at Brenn Head, fixing a seized chipper for a bloke who does tree lopping. Thought it was a perfect opportunity to swing by.' There was a slight pause. 'But I am thinking of coming to live down this way.' He looked at his hands. 'Thinking about it.'

His mum and dad looked at Mike. Dad's mouth was slightly open.

'Mike ...' he said. 'When? *Why*? I thought you liked it up in the city. There's not all that much to do down here, mate.'

'I'd need to get some work. Seen any job ads for an itinerant plant mechanic lately?' He laughed.

Sam swallowed the warm, thick milk of his hot chocolate and kept hold of the cup to warm his fingers. He was getting that funny feeling in his bum, and he held on to the cup tight. It was tingling like it did when he lay in bed at night listening to Mum and Dad arguing. Sometimes he'd sneak out of his bedroom and down the hall to catch a look at their faces, to see exactly how angry they were, if they might stop soon.

He told his bum to shut up. It was all okay, they were all sitting around now, laughing, right?

8

Ferg hadn't slept. He'd stewed all night. And when he'd told Pip over their morning brew the news about Mike possibly moving down, she'd lit up. And Ferg felt like he was twelve again. Of *course* she'd be glad to have Mike down here; he was her son too. That thing of Pip being closer to Mike than to him, that was just a hangover from when they were kids. *I was a little shit, then,* Ferg thought. *Fair enough if Mum thought I was a pain in the arse.* That was when things were still on even ground for Mike, before he'd changed course. It really seemed like that, when he and Liza had talked about it, tried to figure it out; it was like a boat changing direction, straying from its plotted course, being blown by shifting winds. For the hell of it? Maybe. He was smart, that was for sure. Mike had always bettered Ferg at school, got top marks and slaps on the back from the old man. It didn't matter in the end. Fergus had spent good time with the old man before he died, and they'd had Pip living with them for years now; he knew those were good things, important things. He thought they were, anyway. Maybe they were just bullshit. Mike had hurt the folks – not out of malice, of course, but out of pure fucking selfishness – and Pip still thought the sun shone out of him, never said a word against him. Maybe if she knew the truth, he'd often thought, but they'd promised never to tell her; it'd be the end of Pip discovering something like that about one of her boys.

Ferg held a scrap of old netting over a hole in their main net for the orchard, and cut it to size. He wasn't sure how best to secure it. A stapler? Wire? Gaffer tape? Yeah, gaffer tape, that fixed everything.

It felt awful to relive old jealousies. The thoughts corrupted you, scored your insides, and he knew he had to just let it be. Maybe it was part of why he'd only wanted one kid, one Sam. So he couldn't slip into that himself, as a father, being closer to one child than the other – so cruel, so unkind. Thank god Sam would never have to deal with that.

Who knows if you've made the right choices, Ferg thought. *You can't ever know that.*

Ferg reckoned he knew one thing. He had something in him for Sam that he didn't have for any other soul on this planet.

9

Cray's week home was up. He had hardened in the last twenty-four hours, his face less fluid, his mind bringing the desert back into focus in preparation for the coming transition – from Freo, Rosie, their nights out, swimming at Leighton, cooking up meals for the two of them that could have fed ten; to the donga, pressure and stress, extremes of heat and cold, no recreation except drinking and swearing, and borderline inedible canteen food.

'God, and *Shits*linger!' he moaned, closing his eyes for a moment against the thought. Four more weeks, he reasoned. Four more, and he'd be back here, in their bed. And then it'd be time to go again, to go through all this again. 'Bloody hell!' he yelled, chucking the papers against the wall.

'Oh, don't, Cray.'

'Rosie, this promotion, if I get it, things'll be so much better – two weeks on and one off. And I'll get to move out of the donga, too. Never thought a brick-and-tile in the middle of nowhere could look so good.' He let out a breath. 'I bloody hope I get it.'

'You'd better stop thinking about it till you find out for sure, Cray.'

'Yeah, I know. The extra money could come in handy now, though.' He threw her a cheeky look. 'Now that you're a *lady of leisure*. Or is that bludger? Slacker?'

'Well,' she said, 'we'll have to do a few cheap meals, then, won't we? Toad-in-the-hole on Tuesdays, and Wednesdays can be toasted sandwich night. And there's always Mum's best liver on toast for Thursdays. Mmm-mmm.'

‘Oh, god,’ he croaked.

Rosie fell back onto a pile of pillows and cushions. ‘I don’t know what I’ll do. No job. No hope. May as well just give myself up to the Church. Didn’t you know, Cray? *God has a plan for my happiness.* Oh, here’s one – I heard it the other day: *God has no problems, just plans.*’

‘Jesus Christ,’ Cray said, pulling her towards him. ‘Well you know what?’

‘What?’

‘Forbidden fruits create many jams.’

‘Oh. My. God.’ Rosie cringed. ‘You’ll need to take your hand off my boob, then, won’t you.’

On that last night they walked down to the Seaview to meet friends, play pool over a few pints out the back. The pub was conveniently located opposite the local brothel, something everyone seemed to know but Rosie, until one day Marty made a crack about the knocker shop and she unravelled the facts along with some of her naivety.

The Seaview, like its neighbour opposite, was fairly grungy, barmaids still proffering a titty kitty some nights. Other nights there were bands out the back, local outfits trying to break into the Freo music scene. While the old guys drank themselves into oblivion at the front bar, shoving notes down sticky cleavages, the younger Freo crew hung out near the poky stage out the back.

When the band had finished its second set, Cray and Rosie’s group stood around their keg-for-a-table and watched the musos packing up their equipment.

‘Poor bloody drummer,’ said Marty. ‘He’ll still be here at midnight.’

‘’Nother round?’ said Salt.

Cray yawned. 'Nah, not for me. Got an early start tomorrow. Unfortunately.'

'Oh, mate!' Marty said. 'Let's get you back in the water again, four weeks tomorrow, okay? Wash off that mine dirt.'

Cray laughed. 'We do shower up there, you know.'

'Together?' said Salt.

'Not generally.'

'Shame for you, mate.'

'Fellas!' Rosie interjected. 'I reckon I'm getting rather ... *tired* too. Salt, can you get Nat to call me when she has a chance?'

'Sure thing, Rosie, will do.'

Rosie and Cray took the slow wander home through the dark shushing streets of South Fremantle. The walk took them past cottages with clutters of bikes out the front, towering sunflowers and the occasional gargoyle. The conversations they shared on these walks were ones where they thrashed out new views, relinquishing some after a few streets, and settling on perhaps one crucial belief by the time they'd passed the hospital.

As they meandered back to their place, Rosie caught the silhouettes of people moving about their homes, bare feet padding over floorboards, quiet conversations, bedrooms with lights out and children sleeping.

10

When Cray gave Rosie a boogie board for her birthday three years ago, her folks had decided this infatuation of hers with this surfing, fishing bloke was just that: a passing fixation. Never in her life had she shown any special interest in the ocean, let alone in long-haired unemployed specimens obsessed with waves. They were sure the relationship wouldn't last, even though they kind of liked him – he was gentle, friendly, polite. Older. A bit too old for her, they thought; how could you still 'be into' surfing at thirty? Cray liked red wine a bit too much, didn't bother wearing shoes – his thongs didn't count, of course. Just not the kind of guy they'd expected Rosie to love. They had fixed ideas about the way things should be. Rosie could just imagine how they were going to react to the news about her job. She could see their reaction a mile away.

Kneeling down beside the phone, Rosie hesitated. If she didn't ring them she'd have that bit longer with just Cray around her. She looked across at the weekend papers, separated into their sections, fanned around the fireplace where the two of them had sat last night, and pressed the combination of the phone's rubbery buttons.

'Hi, Mum.'

'Hello, Rosie. How are you? Has Ray gone back?'

They never called him Cray, even though it was the only way she ever referred to him.

'Yeah, he left a couple of hours ago,' she lied lightly, letting it go. 'Just thought I'd ring and say hi to you and Dad. How're things?'

The conversation followed its usual format until the point where Rosie couldn't delay telling them any longer.

'What? You did *what*?'

'Dad, I wasn't happy there.'

'But you've only been there a year!'

'It wasn't me; it's not what I want to do, okay? There's no point plodding on with it, it was just a waste of time.'

'But it's your first real job, Rosie, it was a *break*. And what with unemployment rates ...'

'I know, I really do. But it's a farce, that job – all those stories on ... don't tell me you thought it was high-end journalism.'

'It doesn't have to be, for Christ's sake; it's work. It's money. I knew it wasn't exactly what you'd hoped for, but it would have led to something better eventually. What on earth will you do now?'

Oh, god. There was no point explaining any of this. The house seemed to expand around her, the walls started to slide away, and Cray was gone. Why had she given in to her moment of weakness and rung?

'Don't worry, Dad, please, there's nothing to worry about. We've got money saved, so don't think about that.' She paused, trying to express something that was kicking out of her. 'But do you understand ... about the job, why I left? You've got to trust me, Dad. This isn't about money, you know?'

She was stuck. Caught in the process of moving away from saying what her parents wanted to hear – she knew the content and the delivery, man, did she ever – towards what she actually wanted to say. And if ever she gave it a go, expressed her genuine opinion on something, her old man had the habit of making the comment: 'You never used to think this way.'

Of course I didn't! she wanted to shout. *I've bloody well grown up, and guess what? I've changed. I actually don't agree with much of what you and Mum think anymore!*

He sighed loudly. 'Well, love, it's your life, isn't it. It's up to you what you do.'

11

Liza came into the kitchen to see Ferg clutching an avocado. There was a pile of vegie offcuts beside the chopping board. Ferg gripped the fruit and ran the knife through its guts.

'Can I help?'

He didn't look up.

'Hell-o-o-ww …' She was still a bit hyper from another visit from Mike that afternoon – twice in one week! – and had been kicking the footy around in the wind with Sam. 'Ferg! Speak to me. What's up?'

The salad was finished. He scooped up the scraps for the worm farm with both hands, crushing them.

'Thanks for doing dinner,' she tried.

'Maybe I should do enough for five, now that Mike's gunna be here all the time. Popping in. *Moving* in.'

She was surprised by his tone. 'He just wanted to drop that computer magazine off for Sam. I thought it was nice of him. Beyond that, I reckon he's all talk, your brother. He'll never come down, not for long, anyway.' Liza paused. 'It'd be fun for Sam, though, someone else to hang out with.'

Ferg's head snapped up. His eyes were dark. 'Sam's got plenty of people to spend time with – good people. I don't want him mixing too much with Mike, I don't like the idea.'

'Fergus! He's your brother.'

He became intensely preoccupied with a slab of salmon, and she waited there a moment, staring at the chopping board, before leaving him to it.

Later, Ferg went outside into the warm wind. Liza was trawling recipe books, his mum was in bed already and Sam was in his room, at his computer. Most nights were spent like that, either around the telly or each pottering around doing their own thing. Ferg liked it that way, was never one for going out, socialising. Not much good at chitchat, he thought now, as the wind found its way into the marri's highest branches, husking them together like a sudden flurry of maracas.

Despite the wind, stars salted the dark sky, and Fergus noticed first, as always, the startling brightness of Venus, fairly glowing compared with its smaller companions. 'But that's cos it's a planet, Dad, not a star,' Sam had reminded him once before when he'd made the observation.

His own father had shown Venus to Ferg when he was little, when the house was on its own out here in the middle of the forest, with only a few paddocks cleared like the burn marks of meteorites. Jack had built the cottages for the single blokes who'd worked on the farm, milking, looking after the cows. When he retired, he and Pip moved into the more comfortable one, and Ferg and Liza moved into the farmhouse to run the property. They sold the other cottage to Mrs Perry, along with a couple of acres, to help get a start on the blue gums. It was only after Jack died that Pip moved back in with them, into the main house.

Ferg had worried over the decision to expand into blue-gum farming, over the changes it would bring to the property. Part of him wanted to keep the place as it was when his father imagined it, created it, but Jack had told him many times that change was the only way, you had to be able to stay in touch with your children and their children, in touch with their ideas.

Ferg shook his head at the memory. 'Better bloke than me, Dad,' he said out loud, into the night.

A sudden gust caused the marri to strain at the ground, making tiny faulting, shifting sounds, and, although it had been there for years and Ferg doubted it was going anywhere, he jogged over to Sam's yellowed window to take him up on his offer of a few days back to help with pruning.

Liza turned and faced the other glass wall, met its streaked, metal-reinforced pane more for a different view than any other reason; more because she realised that her time spent in the shower was always devoted to the three other walls. Just another meaningless habit, she thought, but the new view was surprisingly different.

She was tired, but she didn't know why. She hadn't been all that busy recently, and at nights she slept well, long and heavy sleep that was difficult to emerge from.

Pip was in bed already, probably engrossed in some sweeping eight-hundred-page historical saga with a box of Turkish Delight beside her. Sam and Ferg were outside with the marri and the torches. Liza thought of climbing into bed with the doona around her and a book – one of the many she had on the go but was too unmotivated to finish – or a good magazine for instant gratification.

'Over to your left, Dad,' Sam indicated with the light of the big Dolphin torch. 'Bit further, yep, that one.'

His dad had the hacksaw out, and was trying to fend off the other branches taking swipes at him as he crouched on the top rung of the ladder. The skin on Sam's knuckles was pulled tight from holding on to the ladder so hard, but the wind was real strong and there was no way he was gunna let his dad come off just because he couldn't hold it properly.

'You alright up there, Dad?'

'Just hang on to that damn ladder. How's that looking? Is the line clear now?'

Sam craned his neck as far left as possible, and shone the torch over without adjusting his grip. 'Um, yeah, it's still swinging pretty close, but it's not touching the line. I think. Can you come down and check?'

Ferg looked back as he put each foot on the rung, breathed out when he reached the bottom.

'Can we have a beer after this, Dad? Like on the Emu Export ads?'

'Sam!' Ferg grinned at him. 'Not with your grandmother in the house, she'd have a bloody coronary!' After a moment, leaning down to Sam conspiratorially, he said: 'But you can have a sip of mine.' He looked back up at the tree, black leaves moving about. 'How's that Vultran guy of yours going?'

'*Valstran*, Dad, jeez!'

'Oh, you know what I mean.' Ferg moved the ladder around.

'Well, he's landed at Sawan and the Sawan people are flocking to Lumptor, which is the last place in that universe that has the red springs they need.'

'And where are they gunna go when he makes it to Lumptor, which is only a matter of time, presumably? Can you hold the ladder again, mate?'

Sam steeled himself against the ladder. 'Uh, I dunno, Dad. Maybe there are mountains there or caves or somewhere else they can hide. And there might be natural stuff at Lumptor they can use against him. Like, I dunno, maybe some biochemical or something.'

'What, as in biological warfare? Sounds serious.' Ferg tapped the hacksaw on a branch. 'This one?'

'Yep, that one. It *is* serious. They have to do something, right? Dad ...'

'Mmm?' He was sawing away. Every minute or so he'd let his arm drop down and hang for a while to refill with blood before shaking it back into action.

'Is everything alright with ... you ... and Mum?'

Ferg stopped sawing. He looked down, descended a couple of rungs, sat. 'Sam, of course, everything's *fine* with your mum and me. We're *all* fine.' He paused. 'How about you, are you okay?'

Sam nodded. He couldn't say anything. His heart was shifting about all over the place. The marri's leaves were warped and bubbling above him. Other people thought they looked diseased, but Sam knew that was just how they were, thicker and stumpier than other, more popular gums.

'How about something to eat when we go inside?' Ferg said. 'I reckon I saw some Tim Tams somewhere in the kitchen – that's if your mum hasn't nicked them all. I'll just finish this last one,' he said, tapping the branch, 'then we'll go in.'

He rested his hand on the back of Sam's head, where his hair stopped. Sam examined a handful of marri leaves, the young branch bending easily to him. Ferg's hand was warm on his neck.

After drying off and smearing some cream on her arms and face, Liza went around the house turning off unnecessary lights and headed for the bedroom. She hoped Ferg would be a little while yet. She wanted to enjoy it on her own – there wasn't much time for that these days, and it was never the same when Ferg was there; she couldn't focus on her own thing with him wanting to sleep, a t-shirt over his eyes to keep the light out. Or if he chose to read, he was vocal about it, his journeys through amazement, amusement and disgust making it impossible for her to concentrate.

Liza thought about Mike dropping by that afternoon. He often made her laugh. He never talked about the usual stuff – work, school, home – even when they hadn't seen him for a while, but picked up on small things he'd seen or heard, or felt. She appreciated that. There was enough of the mundane already. That afternoon, he'd noticed a design of Sam's she'd stuck on the fridge, and had moved closer to inspect it while the kettle boiled. It was Sam's latest X-wing star-fighter design, sporting multiple new features including a secret spot for weaponry and an escape hatch for the pilot. Sam had brought it out to show her after a particularly long spell in his bedroom a few weeks ago. Liza had pored over the drawing with him, asking him to explain all the angles and features to her. *Jet-propelled this* and *hydraulic such-and-such*. It was gorgeous. And she saw, this afternoon, the pleasure Mike took in his nephew's fascination with the technical.

Sam and Ferg came back inside, talking at the same volume they had out in the wind. They came into the bedroom, almost shouting in the otherwise quiet house.

'Actually, I think it's dying down now,' Ferg yelled. He dropped his voice to an apologetic whisper. 'Be interesting to see how the saplings are tomorrow morning, though.' Concern settled on his face for a moment, before Liza distracted him. If he started worrying now he'd be awake all night, wishing on dawn.

'All clear, then?' she said. 'The powerline?'

'Yep, thanks to Sam.'

She watched him, looking down at his son, this boy who learned everything from them, from her, and Ferg.

'Snacks!' Ferg announced, rubbing Sam's back. 'And aren't you looking cosy?'

'We can have them in here, and I'll bring in my night sky chart, because I plotted some more stars the other day.' Sam was off, tripping down the passage to his room.

'Uhh ...' Liza looked at Ferg, looked at her magazine and dropped it on the rug beside their bed with an amused sigh. 'I'd love to see his chart. Better than make-up tips in *Elle*. I don't even use the stuff, so why am I reading about it?'

'Because you're bored, my love.' Heading off towards the kitchen he said, 'Don't let him show you anything until I'm back, I don't want to miss a thing.'

Liza stared at where Ferg had been standing. Bored. *Bored*. Was she?

He was too far away to hear her when she called, 'What do you mean, I'm bored – how can you tell?'

Liza glanced at her rejected magazine. Bored with what? Hurry up, Sam, she thought. Come save me from my tragic life.

Pip lay in bed with the curtains wide open so she could see the sky. In that time before sleep, in varying shades of moonlight, she and Jack had talked about their day, about the days ahead, about the kids, the farm.

Now instead of his voice, she listened to the sounds outside her room, to Liza and Ferg and Sam talking and moving and laughing, or to their silences. Or to the noises from the garden, from the orchard, from the marri, and the night.

12

Paperwork. And lots of it. It should have been a relief, coming in from the sun and dust, the extreme heat. But the thought of tackling that pile had Cray wanting to head straight out the door again. It had to be done. He forced himself to sit. The aircon pumped refrigerated cool over him.

The phone rang and the area superintendent walked in. Simultaneously. Cray looked from the short, bullish figure to the phone as he reached to get it. Shitslinger – more formally known as Don Rittsinger – wanted to talk to him, and he was waiting for Cray to get off the phone he was waiting for Cray to get off the phone, standing too close, not bothering to busy himself with some other task for privacy's sake, but standing there so Cray could almost feel the wave of heat he'd brought in from the site. But on the line was the company boss, wanting to know how Cray's week off had been and could he come in and see him some time this afternoon. Cray felt the movement of his blood for a moment and then made a time with him, trying to sound relaxed.

'Okay, see you then, Neil. Four o'clock. Okay.'

Shitslinger perked up then, listened shamelessly, though there was no way he would ever admit to any interest in that call.

Cray turned to him, scribbling down the time on his desk calendar. He was pleased. He knew it was about the promotion, was relieved not to have to wait any longer. And it meant he could ring Rosie tonight. But best of all it was something Shitslinger didn't have a *clue* about. Pleasant change, Cray thought. How the hell Shitslinger had the job of super was beyond Cray. He didn't have a single qualification to his name, and proudly declared this fact whenever calling someone else a *useless dumbfuck*.

'Don.'

The man raised his brown, lined face in greeting. That was as far as the pleasantries went. 'Have you seen those turkeys over at the pit? They don't know whether they're comin' or fucken goin' – there's about six of 'em hanging around like flies on a carcass – what's going on out there, Edwards?'

He called everyone by their surname, like they were in the army or something. It seemed to be the only way the guy could communicate, if you could call it that, and Cray braced himself for it every time he came back on site. His first beer at the wet mess would be for Shitslinger, or, rather, to get the bastard out of his mind.

'No, I haven't been out there yet, Don. Was just about to get some of this other stuff out of the way. Seems to have accumulated while I was away.'

Don, oblivious to the suggestion that he was a slack bastard, nodded knowingly while expelling air through his nostrils. 'No, I didn't think so. Don't you think you should get those guys organised before you start your paper-pushing, Edwards? I thought you were an engineer, not a fucken clerk. *Efficient* isn't exactly how I'd describe what's going on out there at the moment.'

Cray pretended to be interested in the pages of diagrams and complex maths in front of him. With Don around, he had to hang on to himself.

After a coffee, and after Shitslinger had gone to let fly at a few of the others, Cray drove over to the pit, spraying a fresh coat of rust-coloured dust over the donga office as he left in the Hilux. It was only about a kay away on a good gravel track, and it gave him a chance to see the sky, and the odd saltbush and mallee tree. Tumbleweed raced across the land. Sometimes he'd try to beat it if it was headed for the road, for the car, rolling – almost bouncing – quick and light, towards nowhere.

The guys in the pit looked fine to him, spread out and settled, and no one was picking their nose, as far as he could see. Cray had a chat with the foreman, he was a decent bloke, and asked if the super had been hovering in his absence. The foreman confirmed it, said Dicknose had been 'hanging around like a bad smell'. Cray knew what that was about, knew Shitslinger was gunning for him.

Cray stood next to the truck for a few moments, head tilted right back, trying to make sense of the blue. Where on earth did it begin? He closed his eyes, attempting to get the parts of his life to match up, before driving back to the office.

'It's just a new management approach, it isn't a reflection on you, or your work, Ray – we're more than happy with that. It's about getting new blood into the place, you know, liven things up a bit.'

Yeah, I know. He managed a nod.

'That's why we want to offer you a position that better uses your abilities with the guys, Ray. You're well liked around here.'

Cray was listening. Just.

'Look, we understand that Don isn't ... the best with people. We want you to do his liaising for him, so manage things with the people on site, rather than spending all your time on the technical stuff. It'll mean working *with* Don more, rather than under him.' He paused. 'And of course there'll be some remuneration we can agree on. How does that sound?'

Working even more closely with Shitslinger? How did that *sound*? He summoned up a voice. Sort of. It came out as a choked gargle before forming into anything recognisable.

'Neil, it's not what I'd hoped.' Gargle, gargle. 'It was more that I was looking for ... for a change in the on-site–off-site routine, you know? It gets tiring after a while, the to-ing and fro-ing, it's tough.'

'Yes, it is. It's hard on families.' Neil nodded as if he cared.

Cray thought, *Rosie is never gunna go for this, this isn't better, it's worse, even if he pays me double, it's a shit sandwich.* And managing people with Shitslinger breathing down his neck was hardly going to make the work more palatable.

Neil lifted his head. 'I don't think we could change the fly-in fly-out break-up for you, Ray, not this year, anyway. Perhaps once a system has been set up between the managers, maybe then, but not now.'

Not this *year*? Cray found politeness from a source he didn't know existed. 'You understand – I'll have to think about it, speak to Rosie – my ...' Partner? He hated that bloody new-age, politically correct expression. Girlfriend? Hardly. That sounded insulting, somehow.

Neil nodded. 'Of course, of course, Ray. Talk to your ...' He nodded. 'Give me a ring tomorrow.'

13

Seagulls sprayed into sudden low flight like bowling pins going down on impact. Rosie hardly recognised Fremantle on a weekday. Every now and then the warm salty air blew around her, around the people carrying bags and pushing prams, around the men reading papers in the mall near the two-dollar shops and the ageing buskers, around druggies making calls at the phone boxes while their kids scrapped in shopping trolleys behind them.

Walking along, she looked up to the top of an old white building that housed a newsagent and tobacconist at street level, and saw paint peeling from the walls, windows with tatty verticals drawn, and window ledges moving grey with pigeons, cooing and bustling, and she wondered who, if anyone, lived up there. Or if anyone lived above the pale green undertakers, someone-or-other and sons. *I'm going to be a funeral director when I grow up,* she imagined a small voice saying in front of a class of hopeful astronauts and nurses and firemen.

The buildings were mediterranean against the strong blue sky and were crossed by the white darts of seagulls.

She broke out into the open part of the terrace. Here, Italian cafes lined the street, providing pause for retirees flicking through the *Fin Review* and mums with babies, groups of uni students and artists, and old men who talked around small tables with tiny cups and tight black shoes.

After buying olive bread for her lunch, Rosie detoured around the scene and turned down past Timezone, where bored teenagers loitered and young couples tried to shoot hoops for prizes. She decided to drop into Elizabeth's, have a browse. She hadn't been there since she was a student, when she would roam the shelves for particular titles that would save her a few dollars' precious rent money.

Coming out of there, slipping the old book into her bag, Rosie felt the inherent pleasure in reusing something, in ditching the need for a brand-new thing, the perfect, white-paged, twenty-dollar version. How freeing it was. Somehow, she had an excuse for shabbiness now, whether it was the book, or her clothes, or the fact that none of their plates or bowls matched, and just having to make do. Making do felt better than *wanting* things, so much simpler. She'd almost forgotten, she thought. Of how things could be, how the day could be. The midmorning blue of Fremantle's sky; the strange mix of daytime shoppers. The musty smell of a second-hand book.

When she got home, the light on their answering machine was flashing with messages from Nat, who'd heard the news about her job, wanted the details, and one from Emily, who wanted to know if she was okay. And there was a message from Cray, trying hard to sound alright, but his voice defeated with news about his meeting with Neil. Something in Rosie dropped when she heard him say that there wasn't going to be a change to his work routine, that there wasn't a promotion in the offing, just a move sideways.

Things must be bleak out there, a thousand kays away.

'I don't know what I'm going to do,' he'd said. 'Call me when you get in.'

Rosie sank into the sofa, wanted to think before she rang him back. She pressed on the TV for the company of background noise. This was a habit Cray disliked with a passion. He would mute the volume but leave the vision on. Rosie loathed that.

He must be so disappointed. What could she say to him?

Do a job you hate, just for the time being, until we sort something out; we need the money? After what she'd done? She'd rather go back and work for *The Messenger* than let him battle on with Shitslinger.

God, things were messy now. This had all gone wrong; this wasn't how their lives were meant to be, they were young, for god's sake, they had no kids, no dramas, life should be fun!

She wondered, briefly, if Cray could remember the smell of a second-hand book.

Leighton Beach was on the TV. The newsreader's pat voice.

'... The nineteen-year-old man died last night after being escorted down the Leighton tower by paramedics in a similar attempt last week. The death has angered the man's family, who say he was suicidal but that the psychiatric unit of Southern Districts Hospital discharged him on the weekend, describing him as "low risk". Hospital staff refused to comment today. An inquest will be held.'

The curtains shifted in the breeze. The newsreader placed the page at the back of the pile, looked up to camera, and began the next story.

That things survive — indeed, sometimes thrive — on these dry, smoothed yellows of the sand dunes is remarkable. Arms of succulent groundcover reach and grip. Eventually, waxy magenta flowers open into sandy gusts; insects hide in the calm of the plants' tiny places.

Out here you either resist or succumb to the rushing sand.

A woman in a sarong stands in the fuzzy distance on the beach. She leans lightly into the wind, her weight perfectly balanced, as if the wind were a waiting cocoon, as if she might fall into it and never get up.

14

Ferg pushed through the bush, bending branches out of the way, hearing them flick back behind him. Much easier being here on your own, he reckoned. Having to hold branches wide for people behind you, hanging on to their tips as long as possible before letting go, being careful of where they snapped back – all that was a distraction from things he was looking out for, listening for. He pushed through where the trail dipped away under lower scrub, away from the house, down towards the olive river.

He hadn't been here for ages, berated himself for it when he reached the first rocks where he could see the water, hear the trickling where it broke the surface, reached the banks, found a mossy rock. It sounded like china beads rolled about in the palm of a hand, it was so gentle, so light. How could a sound, he thought, be so kind? He sat, listened, breathed.

Fergus thought about Liza, about himself, about Mike and Sam and Pip. Families. He tried to be objective but knew there wasn't much chance of that. Things had changed over the years. What he'd said the other night was right: Liza was bored. That was why she gave him heaps, he reckoned, in bed some nights when the others were asleep. He hoped that was all it was. He understood – Christ, life *was* boring, generally – but he didn't know how to fix it for her. The mundaneness, the everyday, every day. Maybe it got her down more than she realised. She'd get bogged down in little things, things that didn't matter. There was often tension before they fell asleep. They rarely had sex anymore. It had just petered out, really. They'd talked about it a couple of times, and that was excruciating. They knew they both needed to try harder to keep it all together.

But he was bored too, if he was honest. Underwhelmed. Still on the farm, following his old man's dream. He tried to think. Had it ever become his own dream?

They all seemed to be in a sort of slumber – all of them except Sam – shuffling through the days, not doing much, not caring for much, not caring for each other much, well, not enough, anyway. He didn't want Sam to think it was okay, all this. They had to snap out of it, sort their shit out – but it was so hard to change some things. He wearied. Thinking only created something he then had to try to sort out.

Down below, wind rippled across the skin of the river. Something leapt out of the water, twisting and flapping, then re-entered the water. Silent.

The fish powers through the water, past strands of weed and smaller fish. It darts away from streaks of light that waver with every movement; light siamese to the water's every shudder. Down, down towards slimy rocks and silt, a sprint to elude the thing slipstreaming its tail — and then up, breaking through into the harsh light, fighting its way through the long, weighty moment until the curve returns it, softly, smoothly, into the murky world of the river.

The man looks up, surprised at the sound of the breaking water, catches the limey silver lines of freedom, and fear.

15

It was just before closing time when Mike reached the chemist on the highway. He'd stuck with the place because he liked Annemarie, the pharmacist, and because it was reasonably far from where he lived.

He walked towards the counter at the back. There were a couple of other people in there, mums buying Panadol, tampons, cough mixture, Combantrin.

'Come through, Mike,' Annemarie called, ushering him towards the office, where she let him take his daily dose, rather than making him stand in front of everyone in the shop, swilling the stuff down like a naughty kid.

'Thanks,' he said. 'Have you had a good day?'

'Yeah, busy. The usual.' She smiled.

He'd asked her out, once – she was so vibrant and gorgeous, and they always had a bit of a chat when he went in – but she'd said she was married. 'Yeah, so am I,' he'd replied, amused but not exactly laughing. Married, still. Even though he hadn't seen his wife for years. She'd never come back from overseas. He didn't blame her, either.

He'd had to wonder: *was* Annemarie married, or was that just an excuse to bring the conversation to a rapid close? Really, what kind of intelligent, well-adjusted woman would ever want to go out with a junkie?

He swallowed the sweetened-up syrup. Annemarie always mixed it with a little cordial for him; it was too much, otherwise. Even after all this time, he couldn't stand the taste. He tried not to let it touch his teeth, the stuff rotted them away, dried up your saliva. Terrible, that he was here, how he got here. But he was luckier than some, he was on his way down, his doctor reckoned he could be off the methadone in a year. He'd been detoxing for a year already, but you had to take it slow, the stuff was more addictive than the smack. Nice and slow. No stuff-ups. He knew some who were on it for life, couldn't even reduce their doses by a milligram without getting the full-on sweats and runs. The thought of never being free of it. No, he had to keep going well for the doc to let him go down south. He wanted to try to patch things up with Ferg, if he could, do a bit around the farm. They were the ones who'd always saved his arse, Ferg and Liza, and they were kind about it, despite what he'd done, the stress he'd brought to the family. Ferg still brewed on it, Mike knew that, but what could he do? You can't actually change the past. Lord, how he wanted to! He'd hated Ferg and Liza at times – *despised* them – for how good their lives were.

Yeah, he wanted to prove to Ferg that he could be okay too, live well, be ... responsible. He'd never found the time to show the old man, but while his mum was still around, well, he ought to spend time with her. He sure as hell hadn't bothered before.

16

They lay together, trying to summon up something positive. It was Wednesday. Cray should have been at the mine, but things had gone awry. He wouldn't be going back. When he'd arrived yesterday he had rings greyly circling his eyes. Rosie felt sick, tried not to show it, made him a cup of tea after hugging him for as long and as strongly as she could.

She nearly said, *This all means something, has a reason*, but shook her head at the ceiling, remembering a friend once saying to her: 'Those people who say *it was meant to be*, that's just bullshit. These things happen. You just have to try to go on, look ahead.'

Charcoal thunderclouds blocked the sun from their window.

Cray said, 'I can't move, I can't think.'

Rosie felt scared. She pushed it back, diverted it. She made toast, spread vegemite on her piece, marmalade on his, took it back to bed.

He looked clearer after the food, propped himself up against a few cushions, looked around the room.

She turned to him. 'Let's leave – go down south.'

He stared at her.

'I mean, you're there every chance you get. Every long weekend, summer. You could go anywhere on your salary but it's always down to Margies.'

'I know. You mean live there?'

'Yeah.'

The woman next door was clattering about in her garden, shushing the dog when it barked.

'Well ...' He struggled to get it into his head. 'Why would we do that, exactly?'

This. That guy at Leighton.

Cray rolled on to his side to face her, searching.

'To be our own people,' she eventually managed, in a whisper.

'Instead of ...' And he was quiet for a moment. 'Being other people's people,' he said finally.

Rosie let the tears come. 'God, let's do our own thing, live the way we want to live, grow vegies and things. Pick grapes for a job. Whatever! Do something that's meaningful to *us*. I mean, I feel like everyone's waiting for us to *sort ourselves out* and *settle down*, but I couldn't care less about any of that. And I don't care what they think about us.'

Cray's fingers traced the shape of his receding hairline, and Rosie was reminded of the eight years between them. 'But we *do* care, Rosie. That's the problem.'

'It's too late now, isn't it?' Rosie said glumly. 'It's too late to do it our own way.'

She got off the bed, moved around the room. 'We've formed habits, we've already begun to fill the oldies' expectations – our bosses', even! And it's people our age, too – you remember Zoe and Al? I bumped into her today. They've bought a house, Cray, and they're getting married at the end of the year. She's got a *rock* on her finger!' Panic came in shifts. 'We're stupid, we should never have started with any of it!'

She looked at Cray pleadingly, wanting him to disagree, say it wasn't true.

He didn't say a thing. Not for a while. And then he nodded.

'Let's go anyway. Let's go there. Margies.'

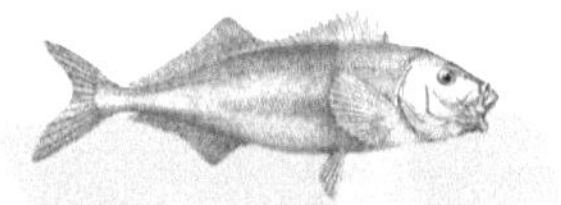

1

The fridge grumbled into the night. Peppermints swished over the roof of the van. Rosie decided to get up rather than struggle with sleep.

All the caravans were in darkness, little curtains drawn on miniature homes. The toilet block was lit up like a late-night diner, and hundreds of insects batted themselves without reward against the white light of fluoros. Rosie ran over in her t-shirt and Cray's boardies, barefoot, avoiding the crippling gravel as much as possible. She chose the cubicle with the best light, read the holiday graffiti – *Sarah R 4 DS, together forever*, that sort of thing – and then relaxed.

The last couple of days had been full-on, packing, storing furniture, cleaning out their place in Freo – a total sweatathon thanks to a cyclone up north. To see the house empty of their things, to let it go. But a relief, too. Shedding *stuff*. Then not to have another place to go to. The drive down south, knowing that it was one-way, that they wouldn't be coming back after the weekend. They were driving into something, and it felt full, like they'd have to carve a space for themselves, rather than just sliding into a waiting spot like they always had in Freo.

They'd decided to relax and look around for the first few days, go for walks in the relative southern cool, and Cray of course wanted to surf. The boards had taken up most of the room in the car on the way down: extra passengers, the rubber-tipped noses pressing into the dash, tails against the back windscreen. Rosie'd had her arm over Cray's favourite board, the rhino chaser, for much of the long, sweeping drive, and had to reach over it awkwardly to touch Cray.

She tried not to think about her folks, their silent

disappointment when she told them. It would just undermine her, get to her, if she let it in. Sometimes you have to be hard, uncaring, or you'll never be free. But what if that's not you, she thought, hardness? Then you're twice caught: being something you're not just to have the freedom to be who you are.

One of the barbecues still had a few warm coals under it, ticking and whispering away as the night grew thick. Rosie looked over at the orange-striped caravan they'd rented, where Cray was sleeping, where they could wake up and potter around, come back to after walks, and where they could read over mugs of tea in the afternoons and cook pasta to keep their bellies warm and full. That van was it. They had no other stuff to busy themselves with. It was so simple.

2

Cray was embracing the opportunity to sleep in. Rosie grinned, thinking she might have to check his pulse soon. She wanted him to wake up but didn't want to disturb him, so she put the kettle on in the hope that the rising noise of it would wake him.

He began to shift in the bed, then made a few grunts, which became slightly frenzied, until he made a loud *uh!*, which alarmed her, and woke him.

'Jeez! Are you okay?' Rosie was sitting beside him on the bed.

Cray closed his eyes against the light and smiled at the sound of coming tea. 'Oh, a dream about Shitslinger – I was ... sharing my thoughts with him. Anyway, god, I want to forget it.' He opened an eye. 'Man, it's warming up in here! What's it like outside?'

'Beautiful. That sound of gravel under people's thongs and kids' bikes – summer holiday stuff. You slept for *ages*. Talk about sleep debt – do you know what time it is? Past eleven! I thought you might be dead in there!' She carefully wound the teabag string around the teaspoon. Clean air cooled across the curtains, across Rosie's hands.

Cray put the paper down. Unemployment and corporate fraud. The sound of TV came babbling in through the window. *TV*. The van next to theirs was decked out to the max, a couple in their sixties doing the round-Australia thing in style. All they needed was a satellite dish and they'd have a brick-and-tile on wheels.

'Birth, school, work, death.'

'What?' Rosie turned around.

'Birth, school, work, death. It's hypnotising, just saying it,' he said, looking outside at the old biddy with a suitcase of toiletries heading off towards the shower block. 'Life according to our parents' generation.'

3

Sam was gunna be late for the bus, and he still had another wet-sponge Weetbix to get through. He looked up to see if Mum or Dad were watching him, but they were talking about something in the kitchen. Sam scraped the sloppy remains onto the cartoons page of the paper, right on Modesty Blaise, who, as usual, was flashing her boobs at a crook. He squashed her up into a little package, pushing it into the bin on his way through the kitchen.

'Okay, bye! See you this arvo, Mum.'

'Have a good day, Sam.'

'Sam –' Ferg looked at Liza, he hadn't had a chance to ask her yet. 'We thought it might be nice to have a picnic down by the river this evening. Do you want to ask Jarrad?'

'Unreal! Can we take the handlines?'

'Yeah, I'll fix 'em up today, after I've been out to the trees. We've got enough reels, haven't we, Liza?'

'For sure.' His mum looked surprised. 'Of course, you know that women are better than blokes at fishing. More sensitive to what's going on under the surface.' She raised her eyebrows in challenge.

Sam and Ferg looked at each other.

'They are *not*,' Ferg puffed.

'More sensitive? What, like the last time we went to Denmark – you only caught buff bream, Mum!'

'You've been reading too many of those fantasy novels, Lize.'

'Well, we'll see, won't we?'

The cat pushed its head further into Liza's hand as she scratched and stroked it, and when she stopped, it opened its mustard eyes to see what other, more important thing she could possibly be doing.

She had the bright red and yellow plastic reels out, and the smelly, sandy tackle box. Puss snuffled around, shoving its nose into the fishiest compartments. Liza loved to fish, to catch just enough to eat, to cook over a fire, to eat the soft flesh. That's why she loved camping. The basics were genuinely basic. They went off in the truck when they could, but it wasn't often enough. They used to go overseas, but it was too expensive for them now. Anyway, all that travelling, Liza thought, all that soul-searching. You could do it in your back garden under the Hills Hoist, find the most serene place in the world next to the agapanthus.

From her bed, Pip saw Liza walk down the corridor with a pile of Sam's t-shirts. On her way back, Liza knocked lightly on her door. 'Pip, we're going to have a picnic by the river tonight, are you up to coming?'

Pip looked up from her book. 'Oh, that sounds lovely.'

'Sam's going to ask Jarrad. I'll get a cooked chook, and make a salad. We'd love you to come, Pip. And it's going to be a beautiful day. Twenty-six.'

Pip definitely wanted to go. She was sick of lying on her bed reading, not that she'd admit it. And she could get Fergus to take her to Jack's ... well, she could visit him, anyway. But she had to be careful about giving those two their space. *After all, it's enough just living here,* she thought. *Poor things, having to live with a craggly old woman.* She'd noticed the two of them talking in the kitchen this morning. Fergus'd said something about *nourishing* everyone, themselves – that was all she caught, her hearing wasn't too good these days – and then he'd held Liza's hand, while Sam sat at the table eating his breakfast.

She looked at Liza now. What would Jack have done? Damn, she missed that man.

'I'd love to. Give me a shout when you're ready. Oh, Liza? Would you like me to make some bread?'

Liza looked up and said, 'Yes – please. If it's no trouble.'

Pip tried to turn her thoughts away from the memories, as blurry as they were. Everything was blurry these days, that in itself was something to think about, how everything had *dulled*.

The memories came back, though, as they always did – like a bad dream comes back after you've woken and gone back to sleep again. They weren't even bad memories, not at all, they were of happy times, times with Jack and the kids, but the act of thinking about those days was painful. *Then*. It was so different from now, her life now with Fergus and Liza and Sam, and no, she wasn't unhappy in this life either, but the distance between those two worlds – the one with Jack in it and the one without him – was vast. A veritable ocean. A world. She hardly felt real without him.

Aargh, these thoughts, these thoughts, they do you no good. Pip pushed herself up off the bed and slowly propelled herself towards the kitchen. She could go faster, but what was the point? She'd always raced around as a young thing, lost no time getting into the orchard in the mornings, picking, trimming, clearing new patches for the next seedlings – Jack had often told her to relax, to slow down, *there's no rush*, he'd say. Now she knew what he meant. There was space, too much space, in her day. There was no rush. Except for the others, if they needed something. Then she'd feel the warmth of blood in her, the warmth of her life.

Pip went to the larder. Flour, salt, sunflower and pumpkin seeds. Yeast and water. She set about making the bread.

4

'I would have liked the gold plating to be a bit stronger. Don't you agree, Fergus? A bit *stronger*. It's a little thin, or pale, somehow, for a man's *name*.'

'But Mum, it's out here in the bush, it's not like –'

'I know, I know, Fergus, but the gold, it's not *strong*, is it?'

Ferg looked around to see if Sam or Jarrad had followed, or found them. The breeze soon delivered him a kid's shout that told him otherwise. He turned back to the stone. 'Well, I s'pose it could have been ... stronger, as you say, Mum. But I really don't think it matters, you know, the good thing is that we have him here, to come and visit, and he's in a place he really loved.' He leaned down and pushed aside fat spears of wild grass, brushed the words and dates with the back of his fingers to shine them up a bit.

Pip smiled, relieved, and rested her hand on her son's. 'I do so miss him.' She paused. 'But now there's you, and Liza and Sam. And that's the way life goes.'

Ferg helped her away over uneven ground. Birds heckled and fought in the trees and insects began the small noises that marked the end of the day.

'And it does go,' she said, squeezing his hand.

The sounds of the kids playing reached them.

'Jarrad, Jarrad, don't worry about those, Ferg'll do them when he comes back.'

Jarrad was one of those slightly awkward but really keen-to-help kids, and Liza could see him spending the entire evening trying to rig up the handlines. She didn't think she could stand it, watching him. *Patience was never one of your gifts,* she reminded herself. Unfortunately. It was probably the best one to have.

The tennis ball caught her eye.

'Come on, guys, how hard can you throw the ball? How hard can you *catch* it?'

'To you, Mrs Crowe?'

'To me, to anyone, Jarrad. Just think of me as the teacher you most dislike at school – try Mr Ridley – and chuck it!'

Jarrad looked at Sam, and Sam nodded his permission.

'Well, let me start with Sam,' he said nervously, 'to practise.'

By the time Ferg and Pip came back the three of them were slamming it at each other, laughing and gasping, in between running to find the ones that were too fast, too hard to catch, and the occasional massaging of reddened skin. Liza caught one from a giggling Sam, and held on to it as the others walked over.

Pip sat down into a fold-out chair and and neatened flyaway hair, smoothing it back. Liza threw the ball to Sam, underarm, and caught up with Ferg as he headed towards the picnic blanket.

'Okay?'

'Yep. Good to take Mum there. Poor thing. Can't believe it sometimes, standing there, next to Dad's *ashes*. How must she feel, looking down at the ground?' He picked up the handlines, fingered them. 'Cleaned it up a bit. She was fussing about the gold plating, Lize ...'

Liza didn't say anything, reached over and crooked her thumb through his belt hook.

'Wish bloody Mike would make the effort sometime. He's never even been there. Never been to where his old man's buried!' He shook his head. 'I know, I know. *He's had his own problems*. Yeah, yeah, yeah. Self-inflicted bloody problems. It just shits me, that's all. And Mum doesn't say a word about it, never complains to *him* about the gold plating. It makes it worse.'

'She's loyal, Ferg, to you both. C'mon, now, good thoughts, good thoughts. Nourish, remember?' She grinned at him. 'Pip's made fresh bread.'

'Hey.' Jarrad jabbed at the water. '*Hey!*'

Sam looked over to see Jarrad all over the place, like he was trying to tame a wild pig, and checked his own line. A little tug. That was just the current, an even tugging, he knew that.

Jarrad yanked away like a crane.

We never catch anything when we come down here, Sam thought. *What's he got?* Dad reckoned the fish here were too smart. Sam got worried one time, thought all the fish, the river, was dead when they didn't even get a nibble, even when they used a bit of the chicken as bait. His mum was cross at first – raiding the picnic basket – then called them hopeless and went to find her secret spot, to *show* them. She disappeared for about twenty minutes and came back with a bream. A good sized one, too. Sam chuckled, remembering. Dad accused her of going down to the shop, asked her where she'd put the butcher's paper. He was spewing, didn't go home until after dark, kept casting out in hope, but he didn't catch a thing. Not a sausage.

Jarrad was reeling in now, the line taut but not really pulling. Weed or something, Sam thought.

Plop! The water broke and they saw a marron on the line. Jarrad started whooping and jumping up and down. His dad came over.

'What is it, what is it!?' Jarrad squawked.

‘A little marron,’ Dad said. ‘You’ve jagged him. Shame. And it’s just out of season.’

Jarrad’s face fell. ‘What, can’t I keep it?’

‘Sorry, mate. There’s not enough of these little buggers *in* season, as it is.’

‘But it’s only one.’

‘Yeah, but if we put him back, there’ll be heaps more next summer, enough for everyone, then. Otherwise they’ll die out.’

Sam turned back to his own line, relieved. It wouldn’t look good. Jarrad didn’t even know how to fish. He felt a bit guilty.

‘Here. Use my line. I’ll wait for Dad to bait this one up again.’ Then he said a little louder, ‘Maybe we need some barbecued chook for this one, Dad, what do you reckon?’

‘Oh-ho, Sam. You’re asking for it.’

His mum rolled her eyes. ‘Having a little trouble there are you, boys?’

‘Nothing to worry about here, Mum,’ Sam chirped. He turned, grinning. The sun was going down in streaks, making her stripey like a zebra. Nanna Pip was surrounded by gold powder as she watched them from her chair. The jarrahs reached up either side of the river, and Sam felt their grand presence, saw how the trees mapped the direction of the water across the land as it moved out towards the ocean, where it mixed warm and yellow at the rivermouth.

5

The woman looked Rosie and Cray up and down, raised her eyebrows and said, 'Yes?' as they stood in the small office waiting for someone to acknowledge their presence.

Rosie suddenly wished she'd worn her work clothes rather than shirt and jeans; the woman wore shoulder pads like a weapon, despite the eighties being long gone. The office was quiet, and a secretary hid behind a computer monitor.

With Cray standing beside her, Rosie gathered herself, raised her own eyebrows in return and said, firmly but politely, 'We're looking for a place to rent. Long-term. Under one-fifty a week.'

'*Under* one-fifty ...'

Rosie shifted her feet on the slate floor. Yes, *under*. 'It doesn't have to be in the middle of town, we're not worried about that.'

'Are you working?'

Rosie's heart sank. Her eyes faltered, but she held the woman's look. She couldn't think of the right thing to say to that.

Cray's voice came into the silence. 'We're not, yet. But if it gives you any peace of mind, we have plenty of savings and good references from our last place.' Cray passed her an envelope containing a glowing reference from their Freo landlords, and gave her a moment to peruse it.

'Do you have anything you can show us?' he said.

The woman shuffled through a few folders on her desk, pulled out a couple.

'Yes, yes, I do. The car's out the back. Come through.'

Rosie and Cray shared a look as they let her take the lead.

The first place they drew up to was a Tuscan-style townhouse, complete with black metal balcony; one of three. *Salmon pink,* Rosie thought. *It's an abomination.* The one next door was *peach.* She couldn't hide her disappointment, a quiet 'oh' coming out as they parked next to the meticulously patterned brick driveway.

Twenty metres further up the road, at the end of the cul-de-sac, was the edge of the forest, with its camouflage greens and hidden sounds. Deep in there, the forest wrapped itself around the river. You could walk straight into it from the end of the road, there wasn't a fence or a sign, just the tip of a brown path.

'A lovely place, really smart inside, very presentable. It's brand new.'

Rosie didn't want to go in, knew they weren't interested, but before they could say anything, the woman was walking towards the front door, almost singing: 'Perfect for a young couple.'

They went in, their voices echoing in the spartan, over-white interior. 'Right, right,' they murmured as they were shown around.

'Could we see the other places?' Rosie finally said. 'Just to get an idea of what choice there is before we make any decisions.'

Ms Shoulder Pads took them to a fibro house on a nearby street, with an overgrown front garden, three wonky wooden steps leading up to the front door and a fireplace in the lounge. Inside it was freezing and smelt of wood smoke.

'How much is this?' Rosie asked.

'Well, it's one-forty. It's had awful tenants in the past. Of course, it really isn't as nice as the villa,' she said, eyeing them.

Isn't it? Rosie thought. *It's much, much nicer.* She could imagine people *living* in it. The street was lined with places just like it, fibro and weatherboard cottages painted light pink, pale green, pale blue.

'Well, it's got a bit of character, and a garden. I prefer it, actually. It's a bit dark and cold, though ...'

Shoulder Pads seemed disappointed that they liked it. 'I'll show you the other one, but it's not in town, it's a few kilometres out, at Greys Bay – do you know it?'

Cray's pupils dilated. Greys Bay, did he *know* it? He surfed it every time they came down this way, discovered the town with Marty when they were teenagers, when they came down with a few mates one summer, years ago. Edge Point, Surge Point, Hut's, Lefthander's. The place was idyllic, tiny, with a beautiful bay curving into the coast.

'May as well just have a look,' he said.

They swung around the road, past the general store where surfers warmed themselves in the sun like geckoes and topped up on energy with pies and choc-milk. The car headed up the steep hill where the people of Greys Bay perched like birds on a cliff, their nests weatherboard shacks sheltering them from the elements. At the highest road – one of only four or five carved into the hill like rice terraces – they turned, houses down to their left, ocean an endless spectrum of blues at the bottom, and to their right land, sprawling wildly away. The hill was a patchwork of coastal greens, yellow, grey, and, where it could, the scrub working its way between the houses. Cray couldn't believe it.

'How much is it?' He tried to sound only lightly interested.

'This one's one-fifty. Greys Bay's real estate is quite extraordinary,' Shoulder Pads said. 'People buy these places over the phone, sight unseen – and they're only fishing shacks, mostly. Hardly comfortable. They're all on rainwater tanks. It amazes me.'

The wooden house was at the bottom of a steep, downwards driveway. On stilts, on tiptoe, the house faced the ocean; the bay curled at the bottom like a foetus, Hut's Beach nestled calmly between Surge and Edge points. When they walked in, Cray passed straight through the house to a set of sliding doors that were moist and misted with salt air. He opened them to a verandah perching over a view so wide that it would need four or five photos, side by side in panorama, to do it justice photographically. He could almost make out the earth's curve at the edges of his vision. The water reached out ahead of him and away to the sides in infinite directions.

Rosie came out, stood beside him.

'Cray.' He knew she was grinning. 'Don't you want to see the rest of the place?'

6

Liza looked surreptitiously at the couple at the next teller.

They were unfamiliar faces, and the bank was one place you didn't get tourists, not inside, anyway. Most visitors just queued up outside at the machine in the wall, even when there were tellers leaning against their section of counter inside, serving no one, swapping weekend stories. Liza could hear the couple talking about opening a new account. 'Curran,' the girl was saying. 'Like the raisin but without the "t".'

Must be newcomers, she thought, wondering how long they'd stick it out. Why was it always here, Margaret River, that people ran away to? Couldn't they find somewhere else to go? Margies was already too busy.

'Liza, could you enter your PIN, please.'

Liza snapped her thoughts back to the bank teller. 'Sorry, sorry, Sarah. I'm in a bit of a daze today.'

'Aren't we all on a Monday.' Sarah's fingers flew over the keyboard, entering account numbers, transaction amounts, her eyes steady on the screen. 'How's Sam?'

'Really well, thanks. Doing well at school. He's clever on the computer,' she said, nodding at Sarah's. 'How are things with you?'

'Oh, you know. Steve's giving me the shits.' She sighed. 'He's decided he wants to move up to Perth.'

'And you'd rather jump under a passing bus.'

Sarah managed a laugh. 'Yeah, well, I love it here. My family's here. Everyone knows us, there's always someone to talk to. But Steve reckons we'll get stuck here forever, me at the bank, him at school. I said maybe, but look at the pros of staying ...'

She opened her hand, ready to count them on her fingers, and then shook her head and said, 'There are so many.'

People walked across the office behind her, folders, pens in hand. A potted palm stood dead in the corner.

Sarah looked like she was trying to stop herself from welling up, and Liza began to feel uncomfortable, and sad. She glanced again at the couple standing next to her. The arriving and leaving. This town. She looked at Sarah, and at Mrs Donnelly waiting patiently at the *Please wait here until you are called* sign, and said, 'If he wants to go, he has to go, Sarah. You never know how you feel about this place until you see it from a distance.'

Sarah nodded weakly and straightened up a little. 'Yeah, I guess you're right,' she said.

As Liza walked towards the glare of the main street she heard Sarah say, 'Yes, please, Mrs Donnelly. Sorry to keep you waiting.'

7

'Kapok-filled piece of crap!' Cray kicked the bed they'd bought second-hand from a guy leaving town. 'The next thing we're buying is a new mattress. A new one, not some hippie snoozer's cast-off. This belongs at the tip!' He punched the sides of the futon to try to spread some of the compressed filling towards the bum-shaped dip in the centre, but only managed to create a cloud of dust.

Rosie was shifting the bits of lounge suite around – armchairs side by side, opposite the sofa; either side of the sofa; diagonally opposite one another – but nothing helped the brown and orange seventies relics they'd found at the salvage yard for fifty bucks. She sighed. Piece of crap. *Piece of crap.* She started singing.

'Cray,' she called, laughing, 'remember that Neil Young song – the one where he just shouts out "piece of crap", over and over?'

Cray was deadpan. 'Never heard of it, Rosie,' he said.

'Yes you have!' She looked up at him. He was red in the face from his struggle with the bed.

He started to laugh. 'Personally, Rosie, I think you're a fruitcake, and I hate this fucking bed.'

Rosie stopped herself from insisting *But you must remember!* and instead went into the kitchen, grabbing a bizarre combination of jars from the fridge and concocting a much-needed sugar hit.

In the afternoon, when she had done all the arranging and rearranging she could manage for the day, Rosie walked towards the open sliding doors, out onto the warm wooden balcony that looked over the town, the ocean, the world. The variously coloured wetsuits at Edge Point moved rhythmically with the water's push and pull, Cray one of them, though she couldn't tell which of the small shining figures was his.

She rang her parents, to tell them about the house, about Greys Bay; to say hello, really.

'Rosie! Where are you? How are you!'

'I'm talking on our new phone, in our new house, Mum – we've just moved in. How are you two?'

'Oh, fine, fine! It's lovely to hear from you. How's Ray? And tell me about this house.'

Rosie gave her the run-down excitedly, was pleased her mum wanted to know all the details, to take the guided tour: 'You walk in the front door and off to your left is the laundry, then you come into the kitchen ...'

Her mum sounded pleased. Rosie tried to describe the view, and their verandah overlooking it.

'You'll have to come down sometime, you and Dad. When we've sorted everything out.'

Afterwards, Rosie was relieved, and felt terrible for the dark things she'd thought about everyone when she and Cray had been leaving Freo; felt like maybe it was her making a big deal of it all along, not them, that she'd got her parents' expectations way out of proportion. And everyone else's. Then she remembered the rock on Zoe's finger, Marty's twenty-five-year mortgage, and she wasn't so sure.

'Life's so complicated,' Rosie sighed to Cray, the soles of her feet feeling raspy-dry against the sheets. She was too lazy to think more specifically about the problem, about *what* was complicated. Often she just couldn't be bothered unravelling her feelings – it was hard work. And it saved her from getting depressed, if she didn't think too deeply about whatever it was.

'Life's not complicated at all,' Cray said gently, turning to her, lying beside him. 'It's we who make it complicated. We fill it with *pieces of crap.*'

They looked at each other.

He shook his head. 'God knows why, but we all bloody do it.'

Rosie farted appallingly. It sounded like a trail bike accelerating. It required emergency action. She pulled the sheets back and flapped a magazine wildly at her bum.

'Rosie!'

She looked over at him. 'What?'

His eyes widened. '*What?*'

Rosie nestled down into the bed, opened her book.

Cray tried to organise some words around his indignation. 'That act of atrocity, that's what! That ... *fart*! I should call Amnesty International – for bloody domestic torture!'

Rosie grinned. 'Don't know what you're talking about, Cray.'

As the smell crept out of the bedding, Cray said, trying not to breathe in, 'We're making a bit of headway in simplifying our life, I reckon.'

She looked at him and smiled. They were.

8

Rosie woke with the dust from the move settled on her face, encrusting her eyes, filling her sinuses. She turned to Cray sleepily, peering out of the one eye that would open. Cray was sitting up in bed, his torso bare. 'You'll get cold,' she said, trying to pull him back.

But she saw him looking out at the gathering and ungathering of the water, and she sat up and looked, too, despite the autumn chill to the air.

The water came in, pummelled the rocks and sand, then retreated. It seemed to woo the land, with an intensity of lines and heaves and movement that didn't exist further out, closer to the horizon. Why is it, she thought, that where the two meet, water and land, there's this struggle?

She flopped back, closed her eyes against the crisp blue day and tugged at Cray. He flattened his cold fingers on her stomach.

'No-o-o-o!' Her eyes peeled open. 'I've changed my mind. Go away!'

Cray rolled on top of her, squashing the air out of her. They lay there a moment, feeling the warmth of one another.

Rosie said, 'I'm a bit scared to get up, in case I don't like the place anymore.'

Cray looked reproachful, alarmed.

She laughed. 'No, no, don't worry, I'm only kidding.'

'I can't wait to get up,' he said. 'I've been awake since about five. Waiting for you to wake up. Since when did you sleep in, anyway?'

'Since when didn't *you*?'

Rosie stayed in bed while Cray got up like a kid on holiday and started cracking eggs rather dramatically in the kitchen.

'What are you doing?' she laughed.

'Scramblers. Up to it?'

'Of *course.*'

She heard him put the things down then, and cross the house to the ocean side. She heard him yank open the sticking sliding doors and the creak of the verandah as he stepped outside. She felt, and smelled, sea air fill the house.

9

Tassie blue gums reached orange tips to the sky. Liza walked in line with a row of young trunks, thermos in hand, wishing the poor buggers didn't have to be planted in such an unerring grid. She stopped, listening for sounds of Ferg: rustling, pruning, muttering. Sam was at home, eating vegemite on soft white bread – his favourite – and browsing on the internet. Sometimes she'd hear the odd *Wow!* coming from his room, and she didn't regret him getting that computer at all. Not as long as they were on the farm and he was still interested in life outside his bedroom; in the river, where she knew he went sometimes before it got dark, though she didn't let on, not to him, not to Ferg. She often saw him heading off through Mrs Perry's place, into that striped evening sky. He always went on his own, and she'd watch him moving away from the house, crouching down sometimes to examine some small thing that had caught his eye.

Mike had rung earlier, in high spirits. The doctor said he could come down, had teed up a nurse at the local hospital to keep him on track with the program if he wanted to make the move. Liza wanted to say *Don't come down, don't come down and get Ferg all messed up again,* but how could she – Mike was family, and he was over the moon about his decision. She was going to need to remind Ferg that everyone deserved to feel wanted.

So here she was with a thermos of coffee to tell Ferg what he didn't want to hear. And she was going to be on his side about it. She would not even insinuate how he *ought* to feel.

She held a foil package lightly, so the heat from her fingers didn't melt the chocolate. Mint Slices, her favourite.

'Stand up, you stubborn bastard.' He was trying to prop up a young tree against a stake, but it kept sliding away and bouncing back to its angled stance.

'Maybe a piece of rag tied around it would make it stay, Ferg.'

He turned around. 'Christ! I didn't hear you coming. A rag, yeah, I know, but I ran out of your old t-shirts the other day. Mmmm, I hope that's what I think it is, and what's that?'

'Yep, coffee. And some biscuits. *My old t-shirts,*' she gave him a death-ray glare.

'They're great for farm jobs.'

'So glad I'm useful for something.'

Ferg let go of the tree, laughing. He sat down on a dry patch of ground, patting the earth next to him for her.

They poured the coffee into enamel mugs, talked about their day.

Eventually, she said, 'Um, Mike rang. Earlier.'

Ferg looked up at her, learned from her face what he needed to know.

'Oh, shit.' His head lolled into his free hand, coffee sloping dangerously in the cup. 'Shit. When?'

'Well, he said he's not sure. He wants you to ring him and you can sort it out together. I think he knows he might be imposing, Ferg, cos he said he'd probably rent a place in town.'

'Good.'

Liza stopped herself from saying anything more. Ferg got up and walked back to the young tree. He yanked the stake out of the ground. 'I'll see you this evening,' she called out, watching him stride over to the truck, rummage in the tray and locate a mallet.

'Yep,' he said, not looking up.

The dull sound of Ferg thumping the stake into the earth echoed around her as she walked back to the house.

10

When the boys were small, Pip carried them over to the orange tree in baskets, and left them under there in the shade like babes in a bible story while she pottered among her fruit trees. Pip could remember, vividly, talking to Fergus and Michael from over in the apples, as she snipped and yanked at the perfect shapes; how she'd hear the boys' little gargles and squeals, and go over and pick them up, both at once, one in each arm. Fergus was bigger than his brother, but there wasn't much between them, just a little more than twelve months. Her two boys and her orchard – how they'd helped her to survive those early years, those long cold winters, those twelve-hour days of Jack's.

Strolling past the dormant lavender, Pip wondered when she'd let the gardening slip away. She cast her mind over the number of decades she'd lived, the way her joints tweaked when she moved around too fast, and how Fergus and Liza stopped her and said, *Sit down and relax, Mum,* when they thought she was doing too much. Now they did most of it. When had those things become too much? One day? Just too hard? Those salvias needed their old flowering stems cut back. Pip fought back the disturbing thought that actually she might still be capable of these things but had given in to the weakness of age, the laziness of afternoon television and ladies' bridge, of being someone's grandmother, and in so doing, had lost something of herself. She reached down and pulled hard on a clump of lovegrass, releasing a spray of sand as it came up.

11

In the fading hour before dinner, while they were waiting for Ferg to come home, Sam stood by Liza as she read the paper, peered over her shoulder.

'Whatya doing, Mum?'

'Reading.'

'*Yeah*, but what?'

'The world's bad news. That's all they put in here. Terrible stuff. We're better off without it, it's depressing.' Liza flopped the broadsheet over.

Sam said, 'That's like the stuff we do in Social Studies. About other people. They have bad lives, don't they? Poor people in India and places, they don't even have enough *water*.'

Liza looked at Sam. Kids, she thought, know everything, and nothing. 'Come here,' she said, reaching out for him, and tickling him into a cuddle. 'That's true, we are really lucky. We have our health, food on the table, a lovely house, and each other.' She grinned into him. 'Shame about the last one, hey?'

'Yeah. You're *horrible*. You guys are lucky to have *me*. I could be someone else's son, you know.' He poked her in the side.

Liza felt it, would feel that poke for a long time afterwards, and she tried to keep her voice light as she said, 'But we wouldn't let anyone else have you, Sambo.'

There was a small pause then, before Sam got her a beauty while her defences were down, working his wormy little fingers into her ribs. She hoisted him off her, crying, 'Dirty rules!' and he scooted out the door and ran, all the way to where Mrs Perry was watering the hibiscus along the fence.

'Safe!' he called.

12

Rosie went into the hotel to get an idea of whether or not there was any part-time work going, and came out with a full-time position, and heat creeping up her back. She wasn't even sure if she wanted to work there, and now she was completely roped into it: uniforms, tax forms, bank account details.

They could do with the money, though, what with the bond and rent in advance they'd had to pay for Greys Bay. And the folks would be pleased, she thought, slightly grimly. Shit. She needed to think this through. She could ring up and say she'd changed her mind. What about the grape-picking thing? Where was Cray when she needed to talk to him? Then again, she didn't have to think too long over that one.

From the rocks at Surge Point you could almost reach out and touch the surfers. The rocks led right up to the waves, after a thin dusty track that began at the boat ramp and wound through the low bush. You could see their individual take-off styles, you could see where they should be sitting, wanted to shout out *Over to your left a bit!* when you knew they weren't quite in the take-off zone, when they'd hump over the frayed edge of the wave as it carried off some other stoked punter.

Rosie perched on a rock waiting for Cray to turn around, feeling like a bit of a surf groupie waiting for her man to come in, which she was, she supposed. Surfers passed her, heading towards the dark water. Most of them were older than the Perth crew; these guys, and the odd chick, thankfully, were at least thirty, they walked quietly, often on their own, with boards under their arms, leg ropes slapping beloved glass with every step. Most did a few back stretches, balancing on a rock, before paddling out from one of the two entry points. Once in, once slippery black, they paddled parallel with the shore for about fifty metres before turning head-on into the swell.

Looking back, Rosie could see the bay cradled between the two arms of land; between Surge and Edge points, whose gnarly fingertips provided the meaty surf, the glossy water, the turquoise barrels.

She could see the rough gravel carpark, full of half-buggered Kingswoods and utes, and the occasional work vehicle – a long lunch for some.

And up on the hill was their house.

Filling the kettle, Cray shivered. White lines of salt snaked along his skin. Sand coated his ankles like breadcrumbs, coming away with each step.

Rosie shed her thongs at the door. 'How'd you get back so fast?!'

'Was bloody freezing!' he said, heading into the bathroom. She heard the hot water system fire up.

When you saw a sand trail, but weren't on the beach, it would lead you to Cray. Small anthills of sand in the shower could be attributed to him also. It seemed to collect in his hair, in the cuffs of his jeans, in his pockets, in his shoes. It never ceased to amaze them both, just how much sand Cray was responsible for transporting round the world.

A muffled call came from the bathroom: 'Kettle's on!'

Rosie made a cuppa for each of them and stood in the bathroom while Cray finished his shower. She told him about the hotel thing.

'The hotel or the tav?'

'Hotel.'

He opened the curtain slightly, so they could see each other. 'Waitressing or behind the bar?'

'Both.'

He lathered his belly. 'Do you want to do it?'

She paused then. 'Yeah ... the bar work would be fun. It's just the full-time thing. And the fact that it's so soon. We've only been here a couple of weeks, Cray. I should be relaxing.'

She noticed the faint new tan line at his ankles, where his wettie ended.

'Well, we'll have to get work sometime, and it's not grape-picking season yet, so unless you want to work at the supermarket ...'

She grinned. 'I wouldn't mind doing that. Or I could always go on the dole ...'

'Or go to the local rag ... what's it called ... the *Southern Way*?'

She looked at him wryly. 'Maybe I'll see how it goes at the hotel.'

13

Cray tried to keep an open mind about what Marty was saying, when he rang to tell him about the new house. He thought he owed it to him, owed it to himself, to consider Marty's point of view, even though there was nothing he could do about it now even if he'd wanted to; he and Rosie'd signed the lease, settled in, were beginning to get used to life down south.

'Mate, you're looking for something that you won't ever find. Stop struggling, stop fighting it.' Marty laughed, then spoke in inverted commas. 'Go with the flow, Cray.'

Maybe that was it, maybe if he just put his head down and got stuck into it, it would all make sense when he was sixty, when the grandkiddies were bouncing happily on his knee. Maybe.

Cray was sitting on the verandah on an old deckchair, the phone cable nearly fully extended from its jack. He looked over the scrub towards the waterbed ocean. He shuffled forward as far as the phone lead would let him as a set gathered momentum out the back. 'But what's it all for, Marty? Couldn't you think of better ways to spend your days than in the orifice?'

'A guy's gotta live somehow, Cray.'

'Yeah, but *live* isn't boats, swimming pools, years spent getting them.'

'Isn't it? I reckon that *is* living, mate. It sure isn't eating beans for the next fifty years. Money gives you options. Jesus Christ, Cray, Rosie might be twenty-two but you're not!'

Cray laughed at his mate's frustration. 'But, Marty, when you've got that gear, you want more. Possessing stuff, accumulating it, becomes an end in itself.'

'Look,' Marty sighed, 'I know what you're saying, you

freaking idealistic hippie, but I reckon you've gotta provide for your family. What about Rosie, what does she think?'

Cray glanced behind him, to where Rosie was filling in her tax form. 'She doesn't want anything. She just wants to be happy, Marty.'

'*I'm* happy, mate! Just because you're screwed up doesn't mean the rest of us are!'

Screwed up.

'Sorry, sorry Cray, I didn't mean that.'

'No, it's okay.' Cray's mouth went dry. 'That's what friends are for. A bit of honesty.'

'No, no, I really didn't mean ...'

But Cray knew what Marty meant, and was glad – well, sort of – that he'd said what he thought.

'Just come down sometime, you and Caro,' Cray said, eyes swinging over the blue. He wanted to dive into the middle of that hugeness, plunge right in, swim down into that world. 'Stay the weekend, Marty, there's plenty of room. And bring your board.' He began to laugh. 'That's if you can still remember how to paddle, you kook.'

'Yeah,' Marty said. 'Might see you down there sometime.'

Cray leaned back in the chair, looked out at Edge Point. He knew where he'd be in about five minutes.

14

Sam was on the phone to Jarrad when Mum and Dad walked in; when his bum began that tingling, that heating prickling. There'd been arguing and night-time whispering for nearly a week now and Sam had had enough. Even half an hour ago there had been raised voices in the kitchen and when he came out of his room he saw Mum marching Dad outside for what looked like one of her Talking-Tos. They were legendary, and you knew your game was up if you were getting one.

It was great to have a normal conversation for a change, even if it was on the phone. Jarrad's family seemed super normal compared to his.

He looked away from their smudged faces, tried to continue his conversation with Jarrad – they were taking bets on whether Lumptor was going to fall to Valstran, or come up trumps, as Nanna Pip would say. Not proper betting, just stuff that would be a bummer to lose, like Jarrad's basketball cards, which Sam didn't even want – he hated basketball – but Jarrad would be spewing to have to give them away. He was trying to think of something he could safely bet but his folks walked in and distracted him, got him all confused.

'How about your modem?' Jarrad slipped in.

Sam's ear snapped back to the phone. 'Oh, yeah, sure, Jar. My *modem* against your poxy basketball cards – sure. How about Mum's potato peeler? That'd be more even.'

Mum and Dad stopped at that, looked at Sam. He could see Mum trying to figure out what they were talking about, but she gave up and went back to what she was doing before. Which was giving Dad the death-ray glare: the official end of a

Talking-To. The two of them headed towards their bedroom, and Sam heard his dad say something rude. Something about Mike.

Sitting on the fluffy circular rug in his bedroom that night, Sam couldn't understand why, when there was nothing wrong, he felt kind of sad. It happened to him every now and then. Now. He didn't cry or anything, he just felt, well, quiet and sad, and noticed things like the wind on his face and the way the bad cat snoozed with its paw over the end of its tail. They weren't even sad things to be thinking about, but they made him feel sad. Mum seemed to know when he was feeling funny like that, would give him extra slices of vegemite bread and cuddles that squeezed his ribs, and would ask him what he'd like for dinner.

'Chicken casserole!' he'd say, diverted for a moment.

'Aaah, the old favourite, hey?'

'*Hearty* chicken casserole.' His dad would nod. 'Good for country families and growing boys.'

'Hearty chicken casserole,' Sam would say, feeling sadder than ever.

15

Liza tilted her head towards Sam's room. He was talking to himself again, or to his computer, though there wasn't much difference in that, she reckoned. Poor little tacker, things were a bit stressful at the moment. Ferg was dwelling on Mike coming down and she and Ferg had had another big blow-up before dinner. *Sam*, she thought. A brother or sister would've been perfect. Someone to mess around with, someone to go exploring down the river with, to gang up with against her and Ferg. They were a kid's rights, weren't they? That whole *kid* world, with their secret languages and silly humour. Liza remembered it from her childhood – the laughing, mainly. The knowing looks and jokes at the dinner table, the general frivolity; it was all part of growing up, and provided enduring memories. She felt guilty about Sam's singledom (she quietly blamed that on Ferg), but tried to reassure herself: there were plenty of only children in this world who made it through life fine, and Sam was one of them. He didn't have any hangups about brothers and sisters, and what he *did* have was her and Ferg's undivided attention. And Jarrad. They were good mates, and she was glad of it.

She pulled clean clothes from an overflowing basket, and plopped them into piles on the table. *Pip, Ferg, Sam, me.* She'd wanted to try for another baby, years back, but Fergus had thought *the time wasn't right*; he'd wanted to wait until things were *more settled* on the farm and until things were better between the two of them, though he never said as much. If she was going to be brutally honest about it, Liza reckoned maybe she *had* thought of it as a way of improving things between them; she certainly couldn't forget the joy of having

Sam. He was an angelic baby, they were almost hypnotised by him; felt truly blessed. She'd wanted to breastfeed him forever, she loved the connection, the sight of him clamped, half asleep, on her breast. Now he was growing up, he was more and more in his own world, and the unspoken ties they had both known – she knew they had both felt them, they had *lived* by them – were weakening as Sam did what he must, and what Liza knew she must encourage in him, what any happy child must do: pull away from them.

But that was a long time ago, those discussions with Ferg. The thought of another child now was somehow wrong, a jigsaw piece from another box. Things had settled on the farm and they'd grown into their life with Sam and each other and the idea had disappeared, like so many things do, with the passing days and shifting skies; with passing weeks and events that come and go and months and words and years.

16

Liza was trying to fill the kitchen sink so she could do the washing-up, but the plug kept slipping away, opening a little crack that would slowly siphon out the water. She'd move it back into place, making sure it made a snug fit this time, and it would slip away again. Six or seven times this happened, and she watched in disbelief as the cumulus suds lowered, as the water shrank away, exposing the fingermarked sides of glasses and mugs.

She stared at them. Tried the plug again. Twitched in her sleep like a slumbering animal.

Sam clicked on his bedside lamp. He couldn't stop thinking about the astronomy mags he'd bet on Valstran being crushed by Lumptor's army. He went over to his desk, wanted desperately to start up his computer but didn't want Mum or Dad to hear. He looked around the room. Shirts, jeans, boogie board, star maps, rug. Rug. He picked it up and carried it over to his desk, a whole bedroom ecology of sand and dust and cracked M&Ms falling from it in the move. Once the computer was well covered, he pressed the *on* button, and cringed. He could still hear it, the singing start-up, though it was muffled. Could they hear it? Were they still awake? He'd be in huge trouble: he had a science test tomorrow. Photosynthesis and chlorophyll. Yawn.

All seemed quiet in the rest of the house. No furry carpet footsteps or waking groans, or whispered voices – that's what he hated most, he couldn't stand not being able to hear what they were actually saying when he heard that vigorous whispering, always had to creep down the hall and get as close as he could to their bedroom door and catch the louder bits. Curiosity kills the cat, as Nanna Pip would say.

Ferg lay next to Liza, who was flinching her way through another world, and listened to Sam creeping around. He'd never be a burglar, that kid. *He'll be tired tomorrow*, Ferg thought. *Leave him be. If he's tired, he's tired. He'll figure it out himself.*

Whoever had come in last hadn't pulled the flyscreen door to properly. It shuddered with the gusts that found their way along the verandah, that found their way to the marri. The wind, seeking out instruments to play.

17

A bottle of bubbly was top of Rosie's list of things to get in town that morning. She would be starting her new job the next day and thought that was something worth celebrating. Walking past the tavern, she saw the shirtless, dreadlocked, stylised-sunnies guys of every Margies summer, hanging around on the grass, around the wooden tables and benches, with kelpies and staffies tied up all over the place. They came down south over summer and stayed while things were good; three months, maybe six if they met a girl, or if they found a great dope plantation in the forest, or if the surf was really pumping. And the chicks, they adorned themselves with impossibly small shorts and triangle bikini tops, or flowing Indian fabrics, long skirts trailing lightly over the ground behind bare feet. Rosie envied their long hair, their lithe frames, their gentleness.

They weren't the same individuals, but they may as well have been the same people who lay in the same places, in the same sun, from summer through till May every year, when she and Cray and the nine-to-five crowd would come down to escape for a weekend.

But winter wasn't far off, now – the nights were already getting chilly, though the days were clear and blue. And when winter did arrive, Cray'd told her, when the rain came down in one long flowing sheet, unwinding endlessly, the few who stayed migrated inside to the smoky TAB warmth of the tavern, to swing around the pool tables, drinking middies and Jack-Daniel's-and-Coke, wondering where their next buck was gunna come from.

No, those summer hordes would be long gone when the clouds came across the Southern Ocean, sweeping the roofs of houses on the cape, a grey blanket pushing north along the land; once the town had settled back into the rest of the year – the real part of the year – when chimneys got cranking at three in the afternoon, and people ran from one shop to the next, and when the parallel parking on the highway, and the beer garden at the tav, were empty.

'A job already, Rosie,' Cray said, raising his glass to her. 'No grass is ever gunna grow under your feet!'

She laughed. 'I leave that side of things to you.'

'It is something I'm quite good at.' He swatted a mozzie searching for a way through his leg hair.

The sun was setting, and the champagne bottle added an elegant touch to the scene out on the verandah. The liquidy sun weighed on Rosie's eyelids.

'We're going to have to have the folks down soon, you know, Cray. Yours and mine. Separately, of course.'

'If only we could keep it for ourselves.' He squinted into it, focused on the water. 'It's ... perfect.'

Rosie looked too. Silver glitter flowed over the surface, where the sun struck the sea.

'Wouldn't it be good to show it off to a few friends, a few doubters?' she said. 'Marty, maybe? Nat and Salt?'

'I'm not sure we'll see Marty and Caro anytime soon. But the *folks*,' he groaned. 'We'd have to *tidy up*. Throw away the beer cans. Plump up the cushions.'

Rosie thought a moment. 'There aren't any. Cushions.'

He looked behind him, into the lounge. 'Whatever. You know what I mean.'

She did. She felt it every minute. *Keep everyone away*. Ring everyone and ask them to come, to stay with them, to share this. Keep everyone away.

She wanted both. And when it came to her parents, she needed both. Maybe, now, she could show them what she couldn't say.

18

Swan Gold wasn't on tap at the hotel, but it was the beer the old bloke behind the bar wanted. Swan Gold. Swan Gold. Rosie couldn't see it anywhere. Dogbolter, Matilda Bay Bitter, Redback, Guinness: the taps glistened with beading icy drops.

'In the fridge, love.'

What?

'In the fridge, behind ye.' Phil nodded over her shoulder.

She scanned the stock of cans and stubbies. Hahn Ice. Tooheys Red. Crown Lager. Becks. Bloody everything. Strongbow. Sweet, Dry or Draught. She heard the voice of the ad man, gruff, sexy. Ridiculous, she thought.

Swan Gold. She took one out and twisted off the top, put it on the bar towel in front of him. He had some coins spread out next to his smokes. She looked at them, at Phil. Was she meant to help herself, or wait for him to pass her the money? He nodded at the coins. If she'd blinked she'd have missed it. Rosie brazenly reached over and took $2.30 from the pile. She had to do it confidently, didn't want to look any stupider than she already did. She felt the others cringing a couple of metres behind her, but staying away all the same. When she wanted help she'd ask. Otherwise she'd fall into the habit of needing reassurance about every single thing she did. *Is this right? How do I pour it again? This one? Is it $2.30 or $2.20, did you say?*

As it was, she was learning the tricks every minute.

Phil sighed loudly. 'Can I have a glass, love?'

He had a twinkle in his eye, so she wasn't in his bad books yet, she thought, taking a middy glass over. Rebecca was suddenly by her side.

'No, he likes one of these,' she said, putting a smaller,

rounder glass next to his coins, next to his smokes. 'A *glass.*'

'Oh.' Rosie nodded. The three of them stood there, nodding at the result: the right beer, the glass.

19

Cray felt great. It was midday. He stretched out on the couch. His body was coming out of hibernation, thawed by the water, made supple again by all the exercise. He felt more awake, and when he slept, he dreamed. Dreaming had left him while he was out on the mine, apart from the odd nightmare, and he was glad to have it back again. Yep, Greys Bay was suiting him just fine.

He turned his thoughts to Rosie. Her first day at work. He wondered what it was like, if there were blokes on bar stools leering at her. He knew what those public bars were like, and in the middle of the afternoon there'd be a few blokes having their second, or third, beers of the day. Supping companionship.

Rosie working meant it was about time he found work too. Bummer really, he was more than happy to just potter around after an early surf, read, snooze, then enjoy a beer or two on the verandah after a LAGO – the extra surf you snaffled when the wind swung back around in the late afternoon and the ocean took on the look of a pane of molten glass. In the evening he'd cook up a storm – Thai curries, vegie stirfries, or lamb chops with garlic and rosemary and baked spuds – and relax with Rosie and an ABC doco. And Rosie'd just been telling him last night, when they lay in bed with moonlight on the doona and the sound of surf down the road, how good it was not to have a routine to their day – they could cook dinner as late as they wanted and it didn't matter because they didn't have to get up at seven in the morning (unless Rosie was on the early shift). They could watch crappy late-night TV, they could have breakfast at eleven o'clock, they could sleep in the afternoons. Bliss.

But he couldn't let her slave away on her own out there in the big bad world. The question was: did he go for the devil he knew or meet the one he didn't?

Cray looked through the slender volume of the local yellow pages. There were a few consultancies, mostly specialising in land development, subdivisions, that sort of thing. Going around to newly clear-felled blocks, and then compaction tests, septics, drainage, retaining walls; checking out houses for cracks and faults and below-standard design. Thrill-a-minute.

Cray flopped the book down. *Jesus bloody Christ*, he thought. *I'm only gunna live eighty years. And forty are meant to be spent working; forty trying to make money.* People seemed to do anything to get the stuff, and expected him to do the same. And yet they all had those mugs with *Countdown to the weekend* and *Thank God it's Friday* on their desks. The least you could do, he reckoned, was have a job that fulfilled the basic human need of *pleasure*.

The flywire filled momentarily with ocean wind. Cray tried to suck some into his lungs. It was Tuesday. And Thank God For That.

He flicked through the pages to the surf shops, board shapers and suppliers of all things to do with the hallowed activity. Shaping. He'd shaped a few boards in his time. The rhino chaser was beautiful in the water, smooth and fast; he'd made that. He had design skills, drafting, the mathematics of the thing. Could he?

Triple J was on in the background. They could just receive it, after a hell of a lot of fiddling; it was their only link to home, a common denominator. Cray wasn't really listening, could just hear the buzz of music and a guy's voice. He was dreaming boards, Greys Bay, forever.

20

Mike left before dusk, passing paddocks and cows and skies of orange-mauve-blue-violet, and houses out in the middle of acres and acres of flat, exposed land. His old bomb, the Sunbird, was ready to blow by the time he rolled into Brenn Head.

He pulled up in the carpark of the Paradise Motel. He'd always wanted to stay there, pink neon sign with flashing palm tree outside the row of sordid illicit-sex and drug-deal motel units, each with a buzzing fluoro strip above the door. He reckoned the palm tree was the anti-Christ in the hospitality industry: it reeked of desperation.

At the motel reception, which was not so much about being received as it was about being sussed out by the guy who ran the joint, Mike paid in full, as per The Policy. The guy took his cash and said quietly, 'Need anything else?'

Mike took a couple of moments to realise what he meant. The manager was smirking; he knew what Mike was. Sweat erupted at his hairline. It was so easy. Would be so easy.

The sudden cool air outside that reception building had the effect of an icebath on him, thank god. He shook his head like a dog shaking off water after a swim, shook the shithead's smirk out of him.

Tomorrow at the hospital in Margaret River, Mike had an appointment to meet his new nurse. Some specialist in relapse prevention, his GP reckoned. *She'd wanna be a specialist for this hard case,* Mike thought darkly. Would she be nice, he thought, would she be like Annemarie? He couldn't handle some tutting matronly woman frowning at him every time he had to down his sickly dose. Wait and see, he said to himself. No point jumping to conclusions, just wait and see.

The bed sagged in the middle. Mike sat on the orange candlewick cover. Tiny TV, humming bar fridge. He pressed on the telly – Channel Two was showing one of the *Carry On* movies. Unbelievable that they continued to repeat them, unbelievable that he found himself laughing. No: chuckling – dirtily. Boobs and bums and scotch and nurses and stethoscopes. All very Benny Hill.

The bar fridge didn't have anything in it, but that's what you got for thirty-five bucks. He dug around in his bag and pulled out a bottle of vodka. Surprise, surprise. From one addiction to another. At least this one you could do with family and friends.

21

By the time Rosie was pelting along Calgan Road in the Woody it was nearly midnight. Apparently, staff drinks after the nightshift were a condition of employment, particularly when the boss had gone home early. It was a good twenty-five minute drive back to Greys Bay, and she pushed it up to 110. The black shapes of trees kept the curve of the road ahead. Moonlight eked through the break at the sky, where the canopy, separated by the snaking bitumen below, did not quite meet.

Rosie looked out for roos and other cars, pressed the radio button to the sound of Ted Bull – silly old coot, but she liked him – and tried to wind down from her evening. She hoped Cray would still be up, but she wasn't counting on it. He liked his sleep, did Cray. Didn't appreciate late-night disturbances or early-morning phone calls, even from well-meaning relatives (especially from well-meaning relatives). *Hopefully he'll have left the light on for me,* she thought.

God, that sounded depressing, like a line out of some old song on the Ted Bull show.

Rosie stood in the garden overlooking the ocean's midnight blue, its creamy hem reaching across the bay. She breathed in the moist, bush-seasoned air. It was so quiet after the radio. Thick quietness. No urban sounds in the distance, no traffic near or far. No voices, even. Just the ticking engine cooling.

Hearing the silence, listening to the lack of sound, almost made her panicky. Greys Bay was remote. No, she corrected: peaceful. Both, she compromised.

The kitchen light was on and Cray had left her a plate of

food with foil tucked around it, and an 'instruction' about going outside before she went to bed. I already have, she murmured, looking towards the blackness of their bedroom. Cray had this thing about outside: he went out and breathed deeply a few times every night before he went to bed, even when they'd lived in Freo. In through the nose, out through the mouth. This place must be fresh air heaven to him, Rosie thought, imagining him out there on the balcony, breathing, listening to the surf, gauging the wind for tomorrow's conditions.

She didn't really want to eat now, at the kitchen table, this late, with none of the homely atmosphere that normally goes with eating – but she knew she'd wake up starving in the night if she didn't. Cray would have gone out and eaten on the balcony. She flicked on the late-night news, settled down with her microwave-warmed bowl, tucked her feet under her knees. After five minutes the test pattern came up. She hadn't seen the test pattern for years, didn't know it still existed. Maybe the station had a few different ones, she thought, just for variety. She tried the ABC. Accounting class. Shit. That was worse.

'Cray,' she whispered loudly. 'Are you awake?'

Nothing.

'Cray. *CRAY.*'

'Mmmnnnhhhh ... what ...'

She crawled onto the bed. 'Hello, I'm home.'

'Rosie, I need to sleep,' he said thickly, covering his eyes with the crook of his elbow.

'I've just got home from work ... I'm all awake. It was my first day, remember?'

'I left a note,' he croaked.

She leaned back. 'Oh, thanks, very kind of you.'

'And some dinner!' He was waking now, propping himself up. 'Jesus Christ, Rosie! I was completely asleep. What's the story?'

'I'm not tired, Cray! My mind's going a million miles an hour and I just thought you might have stayed awake. There's only crap on telly. Unless you want me to watch the test pattern.'

'God ...' He fell back into the sheets. 'I just want to sleep, Rosie. I left that note ...'

Rosie closed the door behind her. Fine. He didn't want to hear about her day. He wanted to *sleep*. She wanted to know: how could he be tired when he hadn't done anything all day?

Rosie washed her bowl and put the kettle on. She looked sideways at the bowl, dripping in the rack, and imagined Cray putting dinner aside for her after he'd cooked and eaten (on *his* own).

After a moment she made a weak cup of tea, turned off the kitchen light and made herself as comfortable as possible on the seventies sofa. She'd not been able to hear it before, but the heavy rumble of the surf as it struck the sand and sucked itself away again came in through the sliding doors, came right into the house. And between the water and the houses, even closer, she could hear the bush, almost loud with noises still unfamiliar. Maybe there were a few accounting skills she could brush up on, she thought, concentrating on keeping her breathing steady. *Nothing to be scared of, Rosie.* She took a positive mouthful of tea and scorched her tongue. White-hotness travelled from her throat to her belly.

Rosie stood up and moved away from the sliding doors and the strangeness of the night. She flung open the front door, turning on the houses that leaned at the silvery night water.

Shouting pounded in her. Blackness pressed itself close.

Not a light was on. Fifty or so houses on the face of the hill, and not one window glowed.

22

Sam loved the night. Everyone was asleep; the world belonged to him. Him and the stars.

Stars. Weird things. He reckoned they were unreachable, mysterious, something he'd never be able to understand. Not *really*, not properly. What was weirdest was that they were part of things, part of the world, part of this solar system. Earth was a star. Well, a planet. Sam knew from his charts that Earth was just another speckle in the sky, one of the millions of speckles he could see most nights out his window. He wondered if maybe there was someone looking out from one of those stars at this one, this bright one, like he could see Venus and Mars sometimes. Maybe. It was funny, the way people thought of this planet as separate, as on its own, like it was special or something.

23

The next morning, Mike flipped the bonnet to check the Sunbird's vitals. Oil slid down the rocker cover. It didn't seem to matter which angle he came from, he just couldn't get the stuff directly into the engine opening. He mopped up as best he could with a grotty rag he found in the boot – an old pair of jocks – and then eased off the radiator cap.

Forty minutes to Margs. Should he go straight to the farm, or drop in at a real estate agent's first? He was going to have to get work pretty quick if he was paying rent. No more DSS. Social security. *Dole*. He could apply down there if he really needed to, but he wanted to work, keep busy, make a real break, show everyone. Show Ferg. How could he ever get back his brother's trust? Ferg still ground that axe, oh yeah, he couldn't put it down. And why the fuck should he? And Sam – he didn't want Sam thinking he had a no-hoper for an uncle. Mike wanted to be able to take him pressies. Stuff for the computer. Things from Mike.

It was now or never, Mike reckoned.

The old tree-lined avenue leading in and out of Brenn Head brought to mind the marri he used to sit in as a kid to throw honky nuts at Ferg. He grinned at the memory. But beyond that, Mike struggled to remember how it felt to live there before – twenty years ago. Twenty *years*! Before he grew up, before he was who he was now. Before Dad died. Before Mum had white hair and watched the afternoon soapies, before Sam was born. Before he was a user, before Jen left him. The world was different now.

He tried to clear his head. He was bloody starving. And he needed a piss. Why hadn't he gone before he'd handed his key in? Mike didn't want to have to ask that dicknose manager for any favours. There was a bit of bush he could pull into a few minutes from here where he could relieve himself. His hunger would have to wait.

The earthworm pushes through dark, wet soil, searching for decay, something to work on and ingest. It slides against other worms, their bodies half hidden, protected against predators: the New Holland honeyeaters, the magpies and kookaburras. Ants, sometimes. Earwigs.

A coming: feet crunching over sticks. The pink fleshy earthworm elongates, retracts, elongates, burrows. Then: golden spray hard against the tree, a sprinkling of warm moisture over the leaves above.

The earthworm threads deeper down, comes across something soft, decomposing, as the steps retreat.

24

Liza straightened up from the paper. A car. And somehow, she knew.

But he was meant to *ring* first!

She wanted to go out to Mike with smiles, put on the kettle for a pot of tea, welcome him as he stood awkwardly at the door, feet making sounds on the verandah, and she wanted to send him away again, tell him to do it properly, for Ferg's sake, for their sake, for god's sake!, because he said he would, because this was the start, the beginning, the end of all that.

'Hello?' he said through the flyscreen door.

The verandah creaked in the easterly, little tocks of falling seeds and skitters of leaves across the wood.

Liza leaned out, peered through the dark of the flyscreen.

'Mike!'

She nearly said something stupid about door-to-door salesmen, but thought better of it. 'What a surprise!' *Oh, beautifully done, Liza.*

'Well, yeah, sorry, Lize, hope you don't mind, I just ...'

'No, no, of course we don't mind.'

He was holding a paper bag gingerly. She eyeballed it. 'What's in *there*? I'd better put the kettle on.'

Mike put the bag on the table in the kitchen, and then stood at the door that opened out to the farm.

'Pip's in the orchard, checking to see if there's anything to pick.' Liza sighed. 'We haven't really been looking after it, it all needs a good pruning and tidy-up. There's never enough time.' She laughed, but felt guilty about it. The orchard was her job, really. It was too much for Pip these days, though Liza still saw her out there on sunny mornings. Ferg was all day in the plantation, and when Sam was at school Liza should have been out there with the folding handsaw, but there were always sheets and clothes to be washed, shopping to pick up. She wasn't even working, really, and she'd let the orchard go wild. Maybe that was something Mike could do, look after the orchard. Pip'd like that; Ferg too. He used to talk a lot about wanting Mike to be part of it. Talked less about that now. He'd wanted his brother to be part of this rambling house – their family home – with its cool stone walls and original weatherboard (which went from fifty degrees in summer to minus five in winter); its four-sided verandah and noisy old trees; its huge kitchen, and bathroom with knobbly taps; the grassy walk to the river. Mike used to be part of it, until he'd gone and stuffed things up so categorically.

'Well, maybe I'll walk out there and find her. She'll be surprised.'

Liza watched him take his Capstan and walk out onto the side verandah, and towards the farm. *You're not wrong*, she thought. *Pip'll be surprised alright. She's been waiting for this for years.*

25

Mike knew he wasn't going to have a problem with this nurse: it was a bloke. A local guy, probably about the same age as him. Surfed in his spare time, he told Mike. So did everyone in this town, Mike thought. All the cars he'd passed on the way to the Margaret River hospital were rusty old stationwagons stacked to the gunwales with boards and wetsuits, driven by guys going home after a day in the surf, with zinc lips and noses, wide black sunnies.

The hospital building was like an old homestead; hardly the imposing whiteness of the high-rise city hospitals.

Despite the warmth of it all, Mike felt like a loser, standing there swallowing methadone in front of this guy who'd made something of his life, who'd probably gone about his thing without too much fuss or bother; without getting on the wrong side of everyone he passed, the wrong side of his own family. If only he could have his time again. People said things like *This is the first day of the rest of your life*, but Jesus Christ, if only!

Outside, kookaburras broke into their regular evening guffaw, throats pointed to the sky.

After tea Sam had looked hopefully at the bag of doughnuts Mike had brought. But Mum shushed him off to his room *while the adults talked.*

Something about the old men's quarters, the old cottage where Mum shoved all their junk – that's all Sam could pick up from his listening post in the corridor. Mike wasn't saying much, just letting his dad speak, and they were all quiet for long periods, just the sounds of mugs being put down on the table. Even Nanna Pip was in there, she was still up! Something was definitely going on. Normally she'd be padding off around eight or nine, even though they all knew she'd just read or watch telly in bed – the sport usually; Sam heard it when he walked past her room, she'd stay up late with it, with the quiet blare of TV filling her room.

Behind him, through his parents' bedroom window, Sam could see the two stars of Centaurus, the pointers, showing the way through the sky to the Southern Cross. He loved the Cross, the way some of its stars were brighter than others, loved the way someone had looked up at the sky one night and linked them all together, those five stars and their two pointers, like join-the-dots, even though they were light-years apart from one another, from Earth.

The door opened before he could turn back from the window, let alone escape down the corridor. Busted, big-time. Liza looked at him and grinned. He tried to give her the sign, the eyes, to say, *Keep it a secret, Mum! Let me sneak off, pretend you never saw me*, but she reached down and got him right under the armpits, went for the big tickle attack, right there in front of everyone, and he was writhing and trying to breathe when he saw Ferg and then Mike coming at him, Ferg laughing and saying, 'This is what happens when you hide and listen in the hallway, you little scoundrel!'

After that they finally had the doughnuts, all together in the kitchen with sugar on their fingers, and Pip beamed over hers.

'Mike's going to be staying in the cottage, Sam,' Ferg said.

'Look, are you really sure about that, Ferg? I mean it's bloody' – he looked at Sam, mouth full – 'very generous of you.'

Liza laughed a little nervously. 'Don't argue with him, he

might change his mind. Look, Mike, it'll be a great way for you to save some money, and it'll mean you can spend time with everyone, but it's far enough away from the house for you to have your own space.'

'The junk shed, Mum?' Jam squirted out of Sam's doughnut.

'The storage shed, Sam.'

He grinned jammily. 'How long for?'

There was a bit of a silence then, looks flitting awkwardly around the table.

Mike leaned over. 'I don't know exactly how long, Sam. Um. A while. Is that okay with you? We can get your computer set up so it's really humming, if you like. There's some new software we can put on it that'll speed it up loads.'

Sam nodded. That was okay with him.

26

Now that Mike's arrival was over, he and Ferg and Pip could get on with whatever it was they had to do. Getting it all out in the open. Sorting out their differences. *Bonding*. Liza just hoped there wouldn't be too much friction in the process, that it wouldn't be too unsettling for everyone, for Sam. She knew it confused him, this thing with his uncle, saw it in his face sometimes – the affection he had for Mike and the strangeness of some of the vibes when Mike and Fergus were around each other. But Sam seemed to know how to sort it out, had his quiet times and his walks down to the river, and sometimes on his way Liza could hear him chattering quietly to himself. And when he wasn't at school or by the river, he'd be on the net or poring over his constellation charts, craning his head out the window when he was meant to be asleep. Liza smiled. She leaned back against the pillows.

Ferg was brushing his teeth savagely, wandering the corridor.

All this preoccupation around her. *What am* I *doing?* she thought. *What do I do, what's my thing?* All the house stuff, the family stuff, it kept her busy but she had room for more, she knew that. It was a pleasure, running the household. She liked each day, rising with the morning, pottering around the house, making life a smooth ride for Sam, for Ferg. It seemed to take all day, attaining, maintaining, that smoothness.

You're bored, Ferg had said, a while back. *Bored.*

'Mum's happy.'

Liza turned her head towards Ferg, rested her cheek on the pillow.

'Well, she hasn't spent longer than two or three hours with him in years.'

'Yeah.' He sighed, and then went quiet.

Liza watched a spider scrambling between the weatherboard planks.

Ferg flopped down beside her on the bed. 'What a hopeless bastard,' he said. 'And what an unforgiving prick I am. I just can't forgive the selfish little shit for putting us all through that – Mum and Dad ... All that negotiating we had to do with the bank, and trying to keep that part from Mum. God, and remember how Dad's hair went white in the space of three weeks when it all came out, about Mike eating into their equity for smack.' He laughed caustically. 'Fucker.'

Liza didn't want to go through it all again, but she could see Ferg needed to, it was the only way he'd have a hope of moving on. 'It was hideous,' she agreed.

Ferg sat up, his back straight against the bedhead. 'I mean, forging your own parents' signatures – for fuck's sake! I still can't believe it, really.'

She shrugged, helpless.

'And now here he is, back again, like's it's all fucking hunky dory.'

'I know. It's going to be hard. You might have to tell him some of this stuff yourself; get it off your chest.'

He shook his head. 'I get too angry, Lize. I don't trust myself.'

Liza nodded. She understood that.

They both watched the spider, just a little fellow, going about its business.

'Families ... you know, they're the hardest work, my love.

But they're worth it. I think. No: I'm sure. They're worth it.'

'And that's the other thing,' Ferg said, riding on his outrage. 'I feel about eighty years old when he's around. Bad-tempered and rigid and ... *conservative*. Mike's boring older brother. But it's his fault! Everything he's done, it's changed us, made us sort of scared, sort of straight-up-and-down ...'

His face turned to the window.

'That thing with the doughnuts. I never even *think* of buying Sam treats.'

Liza let his silence settle.

'I don't want him butting in, humiliating me. I just can't relax with him around.'

Liza wrapped her fingers around his wrist, held it tight. 'You're not *rigid*, Ferg, you're not. That might be how you feel at the moment, when Mike's around, but it's not how you are with me, or Sam.'

She saw him blink.

'You have to try,' Liza said. 'For yourself, for Sam. And Mike. Seriously, Ferg. You have to sort it out with him. It won't go away otherwise.'

'*We* have to sort it out – he and I. It's not just up to me. I've fixed every fucking thing for him before. Let's see how good *he* is at mending shit that's broken.'

27

Rosie queued at the shire offices to pick up their local licence plates. AU: another stamp of their new identity. While she waited, she looked around the reception area, at displays of plans for new buildings and notices of development. In the local paper she'd read about a land development behind a popular family beach, Nurrabup (locals knew it better as 'Nurries', for god's sake). The vision was on the pin-up board in front of her: sweeping cuts into the bush for smooth black roads leading to mansions that no local would ever be able to buy. Or, for that matter, want to live in. Wealthy western suburbs retirees, yes, but surely none of the community's backbone. Rosie frowned as she tried to make sense of the soft-pencilled drawings, the scaling of the thing. How close to Nurrabup would it be? How low-profile would they make it? What did locals get out of it?

Public consultation, the notice said, *all concerns and suggestions considered. Submissions accepted until close of business Friday*.

Rosie slid the Kingswood into drive and took the long way home. She smoothed down hills and crawled up the other side, passing vineyard entrances – long, winding gravel tracks to sophisticated jarrah tasting tables – and forest chalets for weekend getaways. She turned left at Hollows Road and immediately took a hard right towards the small community of Preston, where the river snaked alongside her, deep below the road. Ten kays out of town, Preston was where the river eventually surged into the ocean in a yellowy stream carrying grommets and boogie boarders, stirring up the granular sand of the town's main beach.

To get out to Nurrabup Beach you had to drive through Preston, into scrub-covered sand dunes and towards lonely limestone coast that offered long right-hand waves at Gas Bay and Grunters.

Rosie turned off before the surfers' limestone tracks, into the carpark overlooking the slightly weedy Nurrabup beach and the ever-popular salty cafe. That was all there was here, an uneven carpark and a crusty cafe that doubled as beach change rooms. She got out of the car and stood with her back to the water, looking over the acres of peppermint trees and smokebush that held the earth down, that provided dark shelters for possums and euros and the occasional scampering chuditch. Rosie could barely imagine bulldozers there, crushing the scrub, transforming the place into a twig-covered dustbowl, a developer's delight. She imagined project managers checking on the site's progress, driving through in Hiluxes, pointing blokes in the right direction. Nervous buyers measuring their seven hundred square metres and examining the views, the slope, the drainage.

Rosie's foot twitched on the gravel.

'That's where they're planning to put the estate,' a voice said from behind.

Rosie turned around. It was the cafe owner, her hair wrapped back in a wide headband.

'How big will it be?' Rosie pointed. 'That whole area?'

'Yeah, going right back towards the caravan park. The plans include a new shopping centre and hotel, if you can bloody well believe that.'

Rosie concentrated. 'But it's not definite yet, is it? I mean, it's open for public submission or something at the moment.'

'Open for lip-service, you mean.' The woman laughed

cynically. 'Nah, it'll happen alright. What the shire wants, the shire gets.'

Gulls rose and fell with the wind.

'If there was a petition or something – would people sign it?'

'Yeah, of course, but ...'

Rosie scanned her face. 'But you don't really think it's worth the effort?'

The woman looked at her. 'No, it's worth it. Worth a shot, anyway.'

28

Three men in their fifties sat around the bar, an almost measured two metres between their stools. They knew each other better than they liked to admit, would occasionally look up from their amber lifelines and say a few words, like:

'Seen John?'

'Huh?'

'John. Yer seen him. Around.'

'Not for a while.'

'Keepin' a low profile, I reckon.'

'Yeah. Keepin' his head down.'

Conversation picked up when the staff refilled glasses or reached for another stubby from the fridge.

'What's been happening today, Phil? You're normally here before three.' Rebecca grinned cheekily as she straightened the glass into the last few mils of the pour.

'Aarrgh.' He lit up another Craven A, adjusted his elbows on the bar. He threw her a look. There wasn't much you *could* say to that.

Rosie liked the guy on the left, behind the Matilda Bay tap. Tony, with greying blond hair, and not so long in the tooth as Phil, an ex pro-surfer, divorced, Rebecca had told her. He'd have a laugh listening to Phil and the others, to the gossip shared behind the bar, might swap a few jokes every now and then, but generally kept to himself.

'Did ya get into the water today?' Phil croaked.

Apparently, every morning Tony took his board out to Margies' main break, paddled towards the horizon with the others. He'd catch a few, wasn't quite what he used to be, but he still got out there, every day.

'Yeah.'

'Cold, was it?'

'Nah, ya wimp. It was beautiful. You should try it sometime.'

'Too old for that rubbish,' Phil snorted, snort turning rapidly into a deep cough.

Tony looked at Rosie. 'The day I can't get myself out into the ocean – then ... well, not much left for me.'

Rosie wiped the bar around his glass. She knew from Rebecca that Tony's ex-wife lived in town with another guy, that there'd been an altercation not long ago on the steps of the post office. A mate had had to pull him away after he'd yelled something along the lines of *You slimy shit!*, with kids and mums skirting the scene.

He tipped his glass towards his lips.

This place, Rosie thought. Not the retreat she had thought it would be. Lives could still be on display.

As they stacked the dishwasher, Rebecca told Rosie about the parties they had from time to time, around glowing branches and popping sticks heaped into a forty-four gallon drum, with cartons of stubbies and bottles of wine and guitars and joints and all the hotel staff, and sometimes Tony would come and get drunk and end up cornering one of them for hours, talking and talking and reaching for another beer, poor lonely bastard.

There was a party at Rebecca's place tonight. 'Why don't you come, Rosie, you and ...'

'Cray,' Rosie helped.

'Yeah, Cray. You two should come along, we'll all be there. There are still a couple of the casuals you haven't met, and the new kitchenhand, Morgs – he's a laugh, he's doing up his bongo van to go on an endless surf trip, he reckons, around Australia – and Anya, though she's a bit of a space cadet. Talks all the time about *auras* and *iridology*. I suggested she try colonic irrigation after the last party, she was crapping on so much.'

They laughed, Rebecca checking to make sure none of Anya's allies were around, although apparently there weren't too many of those.

But Rosie was unsure. Ever since she and Cray had come to Margies they'd been living in a kind of bubble, and Rosie loved it, wanted to protect it. But when you socialised, people would ask questions. *Where are you from? Oh. What did you do there? Ohhhhh. How long have you two been together? And so what does he do?* They would come to conclusions. Like her or dislike her. Rosie didn't want it. And yet it *would* be fun to be among these people: blond sixteen-year-old kitchenhands who talked about carving at the Bombie and Carter's; single mums who muttered about their exes; travellers saving a few bucks and soaking up the mellow atmosphere; chefs forging careers and drizzling red wine *jus* around the edges of plates; uni graduates taking time out before *getting serious*. Her. Cray.

29

'And where were you two last night?' Rebecca was grinning at Rosie, with her worming explanation of tiredness, but Rosie could tell it didn't matter, except that now it was known: *those two keep to themselves.*

Still, Rosie wanted to know. 'How was it? C'mon, what's the goss.'

'It was great, really great fun. Everyone got completely whacked and Tim did his usual thing of strumming a few tunes on his guitar and making up songs about ... *Noelene.*' She whispered, wary of the stealthiness of the manager, who apparently was on Noelene's side, and who snuck up on gossiping staff like paparazzi.

Rebecca looked around, moved away from the kitchen. 'You haven't met her yet, she's the owner, she comes down every now and then. Everyone hates her. She storms around like a little bull, pays out on the chefs all the time. They reckon she slept with—' Rebecca jerked her thumb towards the bottleshop.

'*Rod*ney!'

She nodded, with revolted emphasis.

'God!' Rosie imagined it. 'He is *vile.*'

Rebecca kept nodding, then shaking her head, at the thought of them.

Back from the kitchen with a mango cheesecake, Rebecca slid the heavy plate into the cabinet.

'And guess what else you wouldn't believe ... about Phil, you know, Mr Swan Gold ...'

Jesus Christ, Rosie thought, waiting for it. I hope they don't have anything on me. Better not give them anything to work on.

Meanwhile, Corynne came in and grinned mischievously, knowingly, to Cole. Everyone loved Cole, he was the hotel staff favourite, camp as a row of tents. He was cleaning the milk scum off the coffee machine froth arm.

'How're you feeling this morning, sweetpea?' He grinned back at Corynne. 'How was that little treat I gave you last night?'

She lowered her voice. 'Lovely, thanks.'

He moved closer to her, conspiratorial. 'I didn't have any, but Dave reckons he had a snort and it sent him *intergalactic*. He couldn't talk for the rest of the night. I'm saving mine for a special occasion.'

Rosie pretended she couldn't hear them, kept folding serviettes around cutlery.

Rosie didn't have an after-work drink with the others, wanted to get home before sleep overtook Cray.

But she was still too late. He'd left the bedside light on, had a t-shirt over his eyes to combat the yellow shine. The light was for her.

Rosie clicked it off and closed the door gently behind her. In the lounge room, she sat and watched the bush moths launching themselves at the windows.

30

A couple of weeks passed, days like waves rolling over them. One afternoon, as Rosie came in the front door, Cray was hanging up the phone.

'Who was that?'

'Uhh, aah ... how was your day, first?' He cornered her for a cuddle. 'You smell of pub.'

She laughed, untying her apron and pulling the waiter's friend from her pocket. Rosie concentrated. 'My day. It was fine. The till fills up fast in that joint. You should see some of the guys in there, Cray. Nothing else to do after work but go to the pub. I suppose at least there's someone to talk to there, even if it is just someone behind the bar. Anyway, what about you, who was that on the phone?'

'Do you want to go for a walk?'

'Cray!'

'I'll tell you on our walk, come on.'

Even a tiny place like Greys Bay had to have a park for kids to play on, but Rosie was surprised. 'Not very *country*, is it, an oval with a cricket pitch? More like something you'd find in a suburb, or somewhere.'

'Well ... it's got ocean views and roo poo on it, if that makes you feel any better.'

Behind them, the hill reached towards the fading day sky. Low scrub twitched and flitted with dusk birds and patterned the hill grey, green, yellow. Cray and Rosie followed rabbit paths up the slope, scratched their legs on saltbush, passed gaps in the bush where heads of startled but still kangaroos looked over, finally reached the top.

Standing at Greys Bay's highest point, they saw the view open out to the continuing stretch of coastline running south, huge ocean moving with whitewater against limestone rocks and shelf. The cold wind hit their hair, their eyes. No one was down there, not a soul.

Rosie turned to Cray, with the wind in her clothes.

He shouted through the starting drizzle, 'When the wind's down, you can surf that wave.' He pointed to a heaving mass, the white whipping the water to cloudy turquoise. Tiny pins of rain began to hit their faces.

'Christ, look at the sky! We'd better go back.'

'But your news ...'

'I'll tell you when we're home.'

When they stepped back, on to the town side of the hill, out of the wet, salty wind, warm stillness filled their ears, and Rosie's cheeks glowed. They ran for it, up the steep grey bitumen that skirted the houses, till they met the street that stole away towards their own place.

Rosie and Cray watched the sky through the sliding doors. Inside it seemed stuffy, after all that air. But the violet sky would move on soon enough, and the turquoise lagoon of Hut's Beach once again reflect up at them.

'It was a guy called Gus, on the phone before. He runs a board-shaping place out the back of Margies.'

Rosie turned to look at him. 'Are you getting a new board made?'

'No. Well, I might.' He laughed. 'But I rang him to see about ... work.'

The horizon and the sun reached for each other, the slow release of post-storm colours.

'Work.'

'Yeah. Shaping boards.' Cray ran his hand through the air, his arm cutting a smooth line before the evening water. He looked over at her, grinned. 'What do you reckon?'

Rosie was still slightly over-oxygenated, she thought. She tried to remember back to when they decided to move away, to how impossible everything had felt then, with their jobs, how stuck they felt, how funnelled. She nearly caught it, that desperation, it dipped towards her and then away like a cautious bird, but it was enough to remember the rest.

31

'They're going to think I'm strange with this skirt on,' she said to Cray in front of the mirror. 'I know Dad won't like it.'

'Won't he? Why not?'

'Not Country Road enough.' All the colours, she thought. A bit hippie-looking. And it reached right down to her ankles.

Cray was gone, though. 'A quick surf before they arrive,' he said.

'Don't be long! Can you get back before they get here? Cray? It's *important*!'

The flywire door creaked, and she heard Cray's knee cracking all the way up the driveway.

Rosie looked back in the mirror. Her throat felt laced up like a school shoe.

Rosie concentrated on making the tea not too strong.

'What a super skirt, love,' her mum beamed, unpacking a bag of fruit and biscuits and magazines, putting them neatly on the counter.

Rosie looked at her mum.

'It's lovely, lovely and colourful. Young people only seem to wear black these days.'

'Yes, very nice, Rosie,' her dad said.

'Where's Ray?' her mum asked.

'Oh ... he's probably just getting out of the water, he'll be back in a minute, he's looking forward to seeing you guys.'

They looked around. Her dad tried not to appear impressed by the view but Rosie saw how his eyes hung on it, and how they swung around the room over the furniture, the

TV, the dust, the multiple *Tracks* magazines, the coffee mugs (shit, she hadn't noticed those when she was cleaning).

'Good view, though those sliding doors could do with a bit of a clean,' he said.

She glanced at them. He was right, but was that all he could say?

'And has Ray found some work yet?' he added.

Rosie's mum looked across at her. *Don't mind him,* she winked. *Your dad worries.*

'Well, yeah, I have, and Cray's been talking to someone about work.'

They sat up slightly in their chairs, then. Tried to avoid looking at each other in surprise. Failed.

Don't ask, don't ask where.

'Where?'

'Sugar?'

'What?'

'Do you want sugar today, Dad, or did you bring your sweeteners with you?'

'Oh, no, I didn't. Yes, half a teaspoon please, dear,' he said, sending another look to her mum, who tried to shake her head without moving it.

Rosie carried the cups over, and when she'd sat down, she looked at them and said, 'Cray might be starting work at a local surfboard shaping business, designing boards, and I'm working at the hotel.' And waited for the silence.

They waded through it.

'Well ...' her dad started, 'are you enjoying it?'

What? Had he popped a valium or something? Not: *Where's that going to get you?*

He relaxed his forehead at her look, nodded at her to go ahead.

'Yep. It's not bad,' she said guardedly.

'Well, that's good,' he said. And he settled back to drink his tea.

Rosie and her mum stared at each other. Rosie got the Tim Tams quick smart. Cray came in dripping, enthusiastic, noisy, and the three of them exchanged kisses and handshakes as Rosie looked down at the patterns on her skirt.

32

It was hard to see the original words under the scrawly work of the vandal. Liza studied the poster, finally making out the original: RAID (Residents Against Inappropriate Development). It was an action response group (sounded like a kid's toy, Liza thought, complete with battlezone vaporiser) and there was an emergency meeting to be held that night at the recreation centre. The rec centre was where all the town's events took place, from footy matches and theatre productions to underage gigs for the town's kids. As she walked down the highway, Liza saw the flyers stuck up on the windows of the burger joint, the hotel, the hardware store and the crystal shop, all of them defaced to re-read: RAVE (Residents Against Valuable Employment). Liza laughed briefly; it irritated her that this was clever and funny, and momentarily she felt like ripping it down.

She wandered down to the arcade to pick up the things she'd come for. She needed to replenish their house supplies, since she'd been putting a lot of things into Mike's cottage over the last few weeks – soap, loo paper, shampoo, that sort of thing. And she wanted to get a new pillow for him, since the other one was lumpy, not that he'd complained. She bought a stack of five plain soaps in addition to the fruit flavours she chose for their own shower. Ferg would mutter at the appearance of an effusive orange cake, but she and Sam loved them, reckoned that tangerine and grapefruit were the truest-smelling, came out of the shower and cracked each other up with fruity jokes.

That night Liza wondered what to wear, knew there'd be a lot of the town's hippie community attending (certainly more than the town's farming community), and she worried that she'd look straight, *motherly*, in her gear. Standing in front of the wardrobe, she chastised herself for wasting energy on that stuff – hadn't she got over it years ago? Crossly, she yanked on her most misshapen farm gear, and tried to ignore Ferg when he raised his eyebrows in surprise at her. Before he changed her mind, Liza said, 'Right, where's Sam? Let's go,' and headed out the front door. Behind her, Ferg grabbed the car keys and slammed the door.

Liza rolled and unrolled the sleeves of her shirt, looked over at Sam and Ferg and then around the hall. There were about a hundred seats set up, and people were flowing in, some heading straight for the front rows, others seeing friends and piling into spare seats around them. Two chairs were set up on the stage next to a big silver seventies microphone. As seats filled up, Liza began to notice who wasn't there. The hotel proprietors, she mused. Members of council. Predictable.

After a minute Ferg leaned over and mumbled, 'Uh, what does RAID stand for again, Lize?'

Cray caned the Woody along Rockcliffe Road. They weren't going to miss this, he thought, it was an opportunity to get into the community side of things, to do something useful. He was aware of how much he and Rosie had kept to themselves since moving down, didn't want it to become too much of a habit. Rosie didn't agree, he knew, though she was the one who found out about this whole development thing in the first place, but there was a limit to the kind of solitude she talked about. And sometimes he wasn't completely convinced by Rosie's *What I really want* statements. He flicked on the high beams, lighting up the road in advance, and felt for Rosie's hand.

'Have you heard both sides of the story here, Liza?'

Liza and Sam turned to look at Ferg.

'What exactly is the other side, Ferg?'

Ferg looked at Sam to the left and Liza to the right of him, and drew a breath. 'Yes,' he began wearily, 'there usually are two sides to most stories, guys. But I can see you've made your minds up.' He looked at Liza, shook his head. 'Try to teach Sam the broader view next time, Liza, so he can decide for himself.'

'Oh, really ...'

'I did decide for myself, Dad!'

Ferg nodded. 'Yeah. Okay.'

Liza hung a look on him before the three leaned back into their plastic chairs.

Sam shut his eyes for a moment against the talking and moving around him, tried to bring a constellation into his mind's eye. Just black and the perfection of those clustered bluewhite places.

Across the hall, Liza saw the couple from the bank that day, sitting a few rows over from them. They were talking, looking relaxed, laughing occasionally. Liza looked away, looked past Ferg at Sam, and though she felt a small, empty balloon in her gut, she winked at him. Between them, Ferg drummed his fingers across his knee.

33

Rosie strolled up the main street; she had fifteen minutes to kill before her shift started. The main drag, she thought, grinning, was a classic mix of daggy country-town shopping and alternative gift shops and cafes, punctuated by the heavy roar of road trains carrying everything from massive tree-trunks to tankers of fuel. Heading south, up the slow hill, she looked across the road at the draper's, the oldest shop in town and not known particularly for its movement with the times. Decades-old mannequins posed naked and limbless in the window. Rosie had ventured in once or twice. Marketing tricks certainly weren't employed to get people in. The dusty gloomy place had racks jam-packed so tightly with haberdashery, underwear, leisurewear, sports gear and workwear that you could hardly part it to look. Or it was stacked on shelves reaching right up to the ceiling so you needed to get one of the grey-skirted ladies to climb up a ladder to retrieve your size.

Further up the road was the local Retravision store, which, unlike its city counterparts, sold *underpants*. And garden hose attachments, packets of screws and nuts, gas cylinders, TVs, letterboxes. Out the front of the shop, in bargain bins, were packets of pegs (500s), sets of tea towels, and the loose, unpackaged undies. You could *touch* them, pale blue daisies or racing cars, take your pick.

Then, of course, there was the Rainbow Shop, which sold wind chimes and aromatherapy stuff, gypsy girl clothes, jewellery from Thailand and funky rugs. Incense burned as you entered, and Bob Marley sang mantras from the stereo. The dressing room was a cubicle constructed from hanging sarongs, and in it were handwritten signs mentioning shop-lifting and threatening *karma*.

Free time up, Rosie walked into the hotel, swapping hellos with regulars and staff, tying her apron around her hips. Phil and Tony leaned against the bar, hands on weeping glasses, staring at nothing. They moved a little when she stood behind the taps to survey the afternoon business. A few touros having coffee, the Rainbow Shop woman having an early beer with the bloke from the gourmet cheese factory, Cole and Corynne and Rebecca winding down from their lunch shift, about to approach Rosie for a freebie.

Phil's stubby was empty. 'Staying for another, Phil?'

'Yeah, why not.' He laughed, the grubby sound soon turning into his wheezing Craven cough, sending his colour up a few notches.

Tony chuckled. 'Gotta kill them cancer sticks, Phil,' he said, flipping the top on his own Benson and Hedges Special Filters.

After serving them, Rosie went outside into the sun, to collect a few glasses from the early-afternooners. People relaxed around the wooden tables, sunnies taming the brightness of the day.

A gaggle of kids passed on their way to the river, science teacher heading them up, grimacing enviously to a mate in the beer garden. Catching one of the kids' hats as it flew off the small head, and witnessing an exaggerated tip of his mate's middy glass, he complained: 'Look, that's just unnecessary. I'll be there in about an hour.'

Rosie thought about those schoolkids, wondered if they studied any environmental stuff in class in between growing mould and doing liquid nitrogen experiments. After last night, she couldn't get it out of her head how they had to have a new generation of ideas, how totally out-of-date and inappropriate some of the 'brains' in high-up positions were. How they seemed to have little care for a future beyond their own. She wondered if those kids even knew about what was happening at Nurrabup. Watching them as they passed, though, Rosie reminded herself that these kids were part of a community that prided itself on being exactly that – a community.

She checked her watch. Hopefully the kids would make that teacher thirsty as hell, and he'd be here by half three: Rosie wanted to talk to him.

Mister Stokes was a nice guy, Rosie thought, heading back to the bar with glasses tucked under her arm. He'd said to call him Bernie, but it was that teacher thing – she kept calling him Mister er Bernie. It turned out that he was one of the RAID committee members, and was planning to approach the school headmaster and the parents for permission to take the kids to one of the meetings. 'So educational,' he enthused, 'and totally grassroots. You couldn't invent a better case study. And they'd actually be interested too. For a change.'

Rosie felt glad, said she'd look out for them at meetings.

'Yep,' Bernie said, 'I just have to find the right approach with the principal, that's all. Even if just a few of the kids could come along.'

Rosie's manager walked past, then, meaningfully wiping a nearby table of broken chips and glass rings. Rosie grabbed Bernie's glass, though there was still a little left in it. 'Sorry. Gotta get back to it. Good luck with the principal. Might see you guys at the next meeting.'

34

Gus's call came through a few days later and Cray thought he'd go to the pub and celebrate. There'd been a bit of a spike in demand in the board-shaping business, apparently, and Gus was happy to have him sooner rather than later. It would be on a part-time basis. There would still be plenty of time to surf. Cray wanted to see Rosie and tell her the news and he could have a beer or three at the same time. That morning, all morning, she'd sat out on the verandah with a book, but every time he'd looked over, she wasn't reading, she was looking ahead, at the ocean, at the panel vans and Kingies pulling up at the Edge Point carpark. She'd wandered in a couple of times, quietly made herself a cuppa and went back out again, hardly saying a word. Cray didn't think she was angry or upset – he'd certainly know about it if she was – but she seemed far away, and that worried him.

Later, he'd surfed out at the main break, and it wasn't huge, but a few nice sets came through, and being the middle of the afternoon midweek there were only a few people out, unlike the weekend head count. On the weekends you almost needed crowd control out there; testosterone from Perth dropped in on waves others might have waited ages for, ruining the scene for everyone before they piled into cars and headed back to Perth, declaring wicked surf. *Filth.*

Cray looked around. It was that lovely time between afternoon and evening when the light began to change, the temperature dropped, and the sky juggled the sun and the moon. People sat outside the hotel with cold middies. Through the doors he could see Rosie. She was talking to a couple of old codgers behind the bar. He hoped, fleetingly, that they weren't chatting her up.

Cray's hair smelled of salt. Rosie leaned close to him as she put his beer down on the table, loved that smell. Ocean. Wind. She smiled at him, glad he'd come.

Coming to the pub, even for work, had snapped her out of an odd feeling she'd had all morning. Even though Cray'd been at home, even though he'd been near her, when she looked out at where she was, so far from everything, so far from their family and friends, and her favourite Italian deli in Freo with crates of tomatoes and zucchinis out the front; when she looked and saw all that water in front of her, and the depth of the bush behind her, she saw strangeness all around. Nothing familiar, or safe. Just all this wild land and somewhere among it, a tiny community, and somewhere in that, her.

'C'mon, who wants another?' Liza did, and she wanted an excuse to talk to the woman behind the bar – the one she'd seen at the RAID meeting the other night, the bank couple. She looked lovely, and Liza admired the way she chatted to the regulars, had a laugh with them. Liza wondered what she – a newcomer – thought about the Nurrabup development.

'You're meant to be keeping me on the straight and narrow, Lize, not plying me with beer!' Mike flooded sweat into his clothes, slid into his regular evening drowsiness, the effects of the methadone kicking in.

'Oh, c'mon, it's just a belated welcome-to-Margaret-River drink.'

'Go on, then, Lize.' Ferg did his best Yorkshire accent,

burping. 'There's nowt on telly, so we may as well have anoother, then.'

Sam was trying desperately to convince his folks to let him have one, too – 'Just a *shandy*, go on, Mum!' – but it fell on deaf ears, and he rolled his eyes at Mike, who gave him the nod to have a sip of his when Liza and Ferg weren't looking.

As Rosie was pouring the beers ('and a lemon squash for the little bloke'), the woman on the other side of the bar said, kindly, 'You're new in town, aren't you?'

Rosie looked up, surprised. 'Yeah. How did you ...? Well, I suppose it's not that hard to tell.'

'No, actually, it's really hard to tell, they turn over staff at this place like snaggers at a sausage sizzle.' She laughed. 'But I saw you at the bank a few weeks ago, and at the rec centre the other night.'

'Oh yeah. New town, new accounts. And the Nurrabup development thing, well, I just can't believe that.' Rosie trod carefully. 'I can't imagine how people who've lived here for years feel about it.'

Liza leaned comfortably on the bar. 'There's such a mix of people here, you know – farmers and greenies and families and young people. Not everyone's worried about keeping development to a minimum – there's a lot of jobs to be had out of it.' She sipped from the first middy and said, 'But I might be giving the wrong impression. Last night – there were a lot of us there. It was great.'

Rosie let the tap snap back into place. 'That's encouraging, I suppose.'

'How are you liking it down here?'

Rosie liked her directness. 'Well, it's a whole new lifestyle for us, really. We came down to try to make a break – from the city and everything. Like Perth's a big smoke or something.'

Liza nodded. 'Margs is a popular place for that – for a change of lifestyle, I mean. Lots of room to be on your own, if you want that.'

'But it's still a small town, isn't it, despite that. I mean, once you get into the scene, I imagine it'd be pretty hard to sort of ... extract yourself.'

'Absolutely. It's either one or the other, unfortunately. We keep to ourselves, generally. As much as we can.' Liza turned around to where the others were sitting.

At the next table were the town accountant, a couple of local councillors and the newspaper editor, downing pints of Guinness and eating peanuts and laughing over-heartily.

'Have you met that lot yet?'

Rosie pressed the lemon post-mix button. 'They're in here most evenings. Who are they?'

Liza's face clouded. 'Sharks. Developing their way to the bank. Crooks wearing shire councillor outfits. The accountant's in with them, I reckon. Helping them diddle the figures. The newspaper guy's not too bad. He's the one with the beard. He's stuck up for a few good things over the years. Helped stop a few bulldozers. Be interesting to see what he thinks about Nurrabup. Shame he had to do the dirty on his missus with the seccy, though.'

Rosie laughed. 'God, it's terrible, isn't it? Imagine knowing that everyone knows that about you.'

'I know, and I shouldn't join in, especially after telling you we keep to ourselves. It's just so hard not to. It's such a small place.' She looked slightly ashamed.

'I'm Rosie, anyway.'

'Liza.'

Lining the middies on the counter, Rosie smiled and said, 'Really nice to meet you. Enjoy your night.' She almost added,

Maybe I'll see you in here again, but another customer came, and after that, the moment had passed.

35

On the way home, while Liza thought about Rosie, and Sam tried to see the saucepan in the sky as the car zoomed along the bumpy road, Ferg and Mike talked. It wasn't until the marri came into sight, with its reaching, dark branches, that they started shouting.

While Ferg parked, Liza snaked an arm behind her seat to give Sam a reassuring leg squeeze.

'What you've got to understand is, I *never* particularly wanted to take over the farm. I had no choice – you'd already pissed off with your stoner mates.'

Liza decided that Sam probably shouldn't hear everything they had to say to each other, so she told him to go inside, find Pip. Ferg and Mike went silent as Sam shut the car door and slouched up the steps.

'There's no need to be so fucking *personal* about it, Ferg, it's not like I fucking well set out to –'

'Not *personal*? Mate, are you dreaming? What hole have you just crawled out of? This *is* personal! It's about our lives, and how ours, how our *life*, has been shaped by yours, Mike, by your shithouse choices.'

'And don't you think I know that? Don't you think I *know* how I screwed everyone, how I've fucked up ... I lost Jen, for god's sake. I missed out on spending time with Dad. I shafted the folks, and you all know, and I know you all know –'

'Except Mum, of course, who thinks Jesus made you for a fucking sunbeam.'

Mike nodded with forced patience. 'Yep. That's right. That's something else I can feel like a piece of shit for. And it's all completely my fault. But look at you. You've got everything! Look at you, with Liza, and Sam.'

When finally he responded, Ferg sounded like he could have wept, or slugged him, or both. His words came slowly. 'What about what Liza and I've missed, while we were having to be responsible, having to look after the farm when we just wanted to go travelling and piss off, piss you and Mum and Dad off. Jesus, Mike! We missed out on all *that*. Lize and I missed out on all that stuff you do when you're young, when you *can*. And now, yeah, we've got Sam, and he's ... well, he's incredible, but I don't know what there'd be without him. We'll never know what else we could have been or done if we hadn't had to stay here, while Dad's heart was breaking.'

Liza picked at a loose thread she couldn't even see on her shirt. Ferg unwound his cramping fingers from the steering wheel.

Noise came from someone's throat. From their blood.

The old tree leaned over the house in the evening wind, flung nuts like hail across the tin roof.

Sam's bedroom light went on, and after a minute, the blue flicker of his computer screen.

36

Sam didn't want to go and find Pip. She'd be watching TV, boring stuff, love stories with people twirling parasols and skipping down paths and stuff to make you puke. Then again, Pip stashed chockies in her room, all different sorts.

Nope. Sam shut his bedroom door, felt the air suck out. No trespassers! No one was coming in, not Mum, not Dad, still smelling of eucalypts and beer, and not stupid Uncle Mike. He remembered now, how it had been when Mike was here that last time, how grumpy Dad had been (but he and Mike hadn't *shouted* at each other), how Mum had cooked and cooked until they were all chockers, second and third helpings every night, and how his bum had been in *season*, with its stupid tingling. It scared him, how his bum knew stuff before he did.

There was only one thing for it at times like this. He imagined the black shining screen coming alive with information, colours, things to click on, taking you further and further in. The World Wide Web. It was an amazing place. And he wasn't going to turn his light off at eight. They could get lost. Especially while they were sitting out there in the car arguing like people in movies did.

Sam was going to browse and surf to his heart's – and bum's – content, and he wasn't going to ask anyone's permission to do it.

37

Pip lay on her bed, remembering when the boys were kids, perhaps nine and ten, playing backyard cricket. The Crowe Ashes. The prize? A handful of wood ash from the pit fire outside, sometimes rubbed into the winner's hair. Fergus and Mike hadn't changed much at all since those days. They were still competitive, they still loved and hated each other in the same breath. Fergus would just stick it out at the wicket, knocking away Mike's efforts but not hitting anything too wildly; no showy sixes or broken windows. Eventually Mike would raise the stakes and start bowling aggressively, making his brother duck for cover and causing their father to yell out, 'Steady on, mate!' And Mike'd reach the point where he couldn't stand it anymore, and he'd slam the ball down into the dust and storm off in a rage. Ferg'd drop his bat eventually, and slope into the house for a pear or an apple at the kitchen table. Mike wouldn't show his face again till dinnertime, and it would take him until the next day to make eye contact with anyone again.

Back then, she and Jack were sweating it out on the farm – and trying to stay alive in the dark winters. There wasn't a winter past or present in this town that Pip didn't detest with all her soul. They were long, bitter affairs. As a young wife, she did what she could to make the house comfortable, kept it clean and tried to brighten it up with curtains she stitched herself, fabric thrown across the kitchen table. She remembered choosing the material at the draper's, lugging it back and hiding it until the curtains were finished. The day they were done, Jack came in (he'd been nudged flat against a fence by a haughty cow that day, Pip remembered how he laughed about it) and she had them up, hanging brightly, hems not quite straight, but his eyes lit up and she felt that all the secret curtain-making hours were instantly justified by his pleasure.

She saw the same feeling in Ferg for Liza, though he kept it closer to him. She saw the lack of fulfilment in Mike's life, the lack of joy. Of course, she let them think she didn't have a clue, for it was a child's prerogative to *know* that their parents knew nothing about them.

Pip looked out her window at the shapes of the now-mature avocado and fig trees and remembered how they had begun – seedlings in hessian sacks. She'd never thought they could become trees, offering and denying with perfect reliability every year.

The trick to being a mother, she thought, was what you did with what you knew. Unless someone asked directly, you had to be so careful, you had to tread lightly.

Pip reached for a Turkish Delight, a pink one, and decided to keep out of things. She could only watch her children flounder, as though maybe they were just actors on a screen after all, not real people – her people – just outside, shouting in the car, parked on the farm that she and Jack had built from nothing.

38

Mike climbed over the fence into the plantation, and caught his t-shirt on the wire. *Your shithouse choices.* He fiddled a moment or two, trying to release his shirt. The moon was big and yellow, and cast tinted light over the place. Mike's fingers moved about hopelessly. In frustration he yanked away from the fence, leaving half his shirt hanging from it, and went towards the trees.

Why not. Why not, he thought. *Why not!*

A dip in the ground surprised him, his body dropping awkwardly down in the darkness.

It's what I am. Addict. Junkie. Stoner. That's who I am. Who I have been and will be, whatever happens. I'm no different now. It'll be years, this, years ... it's never gunna be over.

He thought of the pub. He knew he could get it there, knew there'd be a source, there always was, everywhere, you could get it everywhere.

His head was thunder. It chanted, *Why not, why not, why not.*

The Tassies stood straight, dwarfing him. Mike looked to his left. His breath was jagged. Trees and trees and trees, rows of them. He looked to the right. Rows and rows and rows of the motherfuckers. He stank of sweat, like he did every night. Stinking, disgusting, pathetic man. A bird flapped secretly above him. Things bustled in the undergrowth.

In a tripping, running panic under a low moon, Mike stumbled all the way up the river to where he knew – roughly – their father's ashes had been buried. It was the first time he'd been there since he moved back to Margaret

River. He'd been there plenty of times before that, even from three hundred kilometres and a million people away, up in Perth.

The moon came through in shafts. He sat on his haunches, like a child, in front of Jack's stone, yearning for a reprieve from his guilt. His litany of failures. But forgiveness needed to be given, and Jack was gone.

39

Cray woke with the sun rising over the bay and glassy peelers calling to him. His head was foggy from the beers at the pub last night. Greys Bay was quiet, except for the crunch of country roads under early surfers' tyres, and the barking of a dog calling to his owner. There were only three other guys out. Cray could just make out their dark figures straddling boards, rising and falling with the irregular, perfect heaves of the water.

Rosie moved a little, and he got out of bed quietly, pulling on his cold boardies and rash vest. He waxed up his rhino chaser outside, the bubblegum smell of it in his nose. What could be better than this? An unhassled early morning surf in perfect conditions, a couple of hours of 'work' later on (he almost laughed at the idea of board-shaping as work), Rosie to be with, time for another surf later on. He breathed in the cool blue air as he walked down the sleeping dawn street towards Edge Point.

Rosie woke to the satisfied sounds of Cray brushing sand from his board, and the rather less appealing sound of him blowing sea water from his nose. She staggered out towards the kettle, squinting at him through morning slit-eyes in distaste.

'God, you're a bit much. Mister Fit and Healthy and *the-world-is-good.*'

He laughed. 'Yeah, unlike you, despite your tender years. How about we do time trials around the oval and see who comes out best?'

'I wouldn't want to embarrass you. And just for the

record, let it be known that the *only* time you get up early is when the swell's up. Not for anything else.'

But he was too zen after his surf to bite.

Rosie had the day off. Cray's sandy feet scratched over the lino as he dropped slabs of bread into the toaster. Rosie thought she should do something *outside* in her time off. Sitting around the house reading, well, you could be anywhere: Perth, Margaret River, Costa Rica. There was no point being here, coming down south, if you weren't going to make the most of what it offered. Yes, something outside, she decided. Maybe it would help. She'd heard at the pub about the two teachers who'd lived in the house before she and Cray moved in, two women who'd been posted to the Catholic school in Margaret River, who'd left after a year. They'd rarely left the house except to go to work. Didn't go for walks or for an evening dip in the bay. And it wasn't just because one of them had missed her fiancé in Perth, or because the other had had to endure the deputy head feeling her arse after the children had gone home for the day. It was because they'd hated the place. And Rosie could understand that now: it made you slightly nervous, all the space, the lack of people. But she was determined not to become like them, not let the place push her away. When she'd heard that story, Rosie remembered how cobwebby and dusty the wooden furniture out on the verandah had been when she and Cray moved in, a week after the teachers had gone. She'd swept it clean with a small brush, had carefully unclung the grey webs.

Rosie went for a drive, the radio announcer's familiar voice reassuring, and found a beach where there were no cars parked in the limestone patch. Following the path down to the water, she walked over the dunes, hands on Koppers logs to steady her, towel slung over her shoulder. She passed through the creamy dune sand to the coarser shell coating on the shore, felt the shiny, broken pieces dig into the soles of her feet.

She saw the dark blue of the coming wind sweep the sea like a vacuum over carpet, felt her hair pull lightly away from her neck, fly with the air.

In the rock of the headland, among the highest bush and the red crusty strata of earth, swings a falcon, tiny legs of a mouse kicking in its mouth.

The falcon powers away to a cliff nest, a few strokes over the plunging and lifting water beneath, where a pink mouth waits wide, and where the sun comes in golden, late in the day.

It has every view of the world, this bird, and takes in the speck of a young woman on the beach below.

The search for sustenance, the ferrying of nourishment, is now an hourly mission. And so the bird flies, back and forth, dipping and rising, across and through a world, until the gangly, surprisingly large eyas can make its own way out over the cliffs, into the stinging spray, leaving the mother alone.

40

Cray had on his oldest, tattiest King Gee shirt, and his gardening shorts. Worker's green. No sterile business shirt or tie around his neck. (Who *invented* ties? he fumed momentarily.) After all, at this job he'd be working with his hands, with fibreglass and resin. He looked down at his hands. The simplicity of that, of making things. Things for people to use for pleasure, for leisure, to sustain them.

Gus was there, having a coffee with the other, much younger, apprentice when he arrived. Cray was an apprentice too, now, and that was a bit of a worry, he knew, starting from scratch at thirty, but why exactly? As far as he knew, there was no book of rules: *The Way To Go About Life: A Compact Guide* by D. H. Knob-Jockey, PhD. At the end, he'd be lying on his deathbed facing nothingness, and he'd be the only one looking back over this life. No one else would be too concerned about what he'd done or not done. An old codger like any other, he'd have made it through to the end, and how he got there wasn't important, let alone interesting, to anyone else. That's if he made it to codgerdom. He reminded himself of the proverbial bus just around the corner, and slowed his thoughts.

'Want a brew, Ray?'

'Yeah, thanks. It's Cray, actually. Uhh ... it's a nickname from way back, just stuck.' He struggled to explain without going into it. 'From when I worked the crayboats.'

'Righto, mate.' Gus raised an eyebrow in good humour. 'Whatever you prefer. We're used to funny names round here.'

Cray scanned the workshop, at the boards in the making, at the blanks and the vats of resin, the airbrushes and Gorilla Grip, the belt sanders and foam shavings littering the floor like fake snow; at the finished products drying on racks, waiting to be tried out. Each board was unique, a creation of surfer-specific engineering. The thickness and curve of the plank, the shape, number and position of the fins, the angle of the nose: these were all custom-designed to aid the individual surfer's ocean needs, depending on where they surfed, their height and weight, their surfing style. You wouldn't make a Malibu-style plank for a hardcore young guy who was out there trying to carve his initials into the water, to feel the adrenalin zip through his system with sharp turns and avalanche drops, just as you wouldn't make a super-lightweight thruster for a middle-aged bloke who only wanted to go out and get wet, relax into the waves, feel the motion of the water under him.

Just being around boards made Cray want to plunge into the cool, spritzy stuff. Natural exfoliant, Rosie always said about the whitewater. More women should try it.

Gus put a mug of coffee next to Cray, and pointed to a blank.

'There you go, mate,' he said. 'A clean slate. Let's get into it.'

41

Ferg hauled himself out of bed and examined his feet with bug-eyes. That bloody brother. Bloody damn selfish bastard. He couldn't stand the thought of seeing him this morning.

He looked over at Liza. She was wide awake, and looking dreadful. Pale. He sighed. A light sou'-easterly was blowing against the flyscreen. The marri creaked its good-morning. Ferg felt like the oldest person in the world, without the wisdom.

The only person he felt like being with was Sam. Sam would already be up, in his room immersed in one of his projects. That boy was the king of projects. Always something on the go, always something to disappear into.

Ferg pulled on yesterday's shorts, with yesterday's undies in, and quietly went down the hall to hang out with the sanest person in the house.

Out in the brisk morning, overlooking the orchard's bare winter branches, Pip dug into the flesh of the grapefruit, careful not to scoop up too much pith. Her mother used to eat the skin of oranges. The memory of it made her cringe, yet it came with an image of her mother: young, smooth-skinned, and with a bold smile. Pip was older now than her mother was when she died. Her mother had raised the four of *them* without batting an eyelid, it seemed. Where had Pip gone so wrong with her boys? The tension since Mike had arrived was wearing. She often felt anxious leaving her room to join them sitting around the kitchen table, or flopping on the sofas. What was she walking into? Why couldn't they just accept one another and get on with things? There was so much gnashing and wailing these days, rather than just putting your head down and getting on.

Pip rested her teaspoon on the edge of the saucer.

Liza pushed her feet into her uggies and headed out to the cottage. She had in her hand half a loaf of bread she'd grabbed from the kitchen. She wouldn't be a minute, she'd just take him the bread and make sure he was okay.

The old gate door was wide open when Liza got there, and the usual twenty-eights came swooping over when they saw her. She knocked and peered in to see Mike sitting on the side of the bed looking worse than all of them put together.

'Oh, Lize. Morning.'

'Moaning.'

She put the bread down on the table. 'Brought you something for the toaster.'

Mike tried to look interested, tried to push himself from the side of the bed, and didn't manage either.

The twenty-eights squawked raucously from the verandah.

Liza turned to them, started to say something and then stopped herself.

She wondered if they knew each other, those green and yellow birds sitting side by side, pointing her way, beseeching her.

'Come in for lunch, later. If you feel like it,' she said. 'I'm making a big pot of vegie soup.'

Mike didn't look up.

42

Work tomorrow. Rosie was getting bored with cleaning the lines every night, with making takeaway skinny decaffeinated cappuccinos for tourists with nothing better to do than compete for the most annoying coffee requests. ('Do you have soy milk? I'll have a skinny soy decap then, minus chocolate.' 'No, we're out of caraway seeds this morning. Will your long black be alright without them?') The novelty of finding a sleeping Crayfish in their bed by the time she got home was wearing off. As were paypackets with a pittance in them, even though she worked split shifts and her days off were rarely back-to-back.

It wasn't what she'd had in mind six months back when they moved down. The money didn't matter, but it didn't help either. The job was fun but endlessly repetitive. She didn't want to go back to Perth. She didn't want to see another soul for the rest of her life, but that afternoon she waited and waited for Cray to come home.

'It's a different situation now, Rosie,' Cray said. 'Things have changed. It'd be different.'

'Would it?'

He sighed. 'I don't know. You don't know.'

'Just a bit of freelance stuff. To stop my brain becoming slush while I pour beers.' She looked at him, knew what he was about to say, nodded wryly at him.

'*Becoming*?'

'Predictable, Cray. It'll probably accelerate the process,

anyway.' Rosie felt slightly sick. Cray reeked of resin, and that didn't help.

'Don't forget,' he looked at her knowingly, and then duly recited: 'If in the last few years you haven't discarded a major opinion or acquired a new one, check your pulse, you may be dead.'

'Aah, that's right.' She lay back on the bed. It was one of their favourite sayings, got them out of all sorts of otherwise humiliating situations.

'And I can always change. Again.' She rolled her eyes.

He turned the silver ring on her finger. 'You've forgotten the best thing.' He paused, giving her time to guess. 'You don't have to *tell* anyone. No one to inform. That's your kinda privacy.'

She grinned guiltily at him. 'Living in the country, hey? You gotta love it.'

43

While they were waiting for everyone to squeeze out through the rec centre doors (Ferg refused to get up immediately and queue 'like sheep at the gate'), Liza heard a voice behind her say, 'What was that you were saying about sharks?' She turned to see Rosie trying to put words to her outrage. 'You were right, the council's just ... just ...'

'Off, like an esky of week-old mulies,' Cray helped.

'And a local guy behind it – what's wrong with him? It's bloody terrible.'

Liza, so pleased at the friendliness, shook her head in shared disappointment. 'Yeah, you'd hardly think that they actually live here. It's just money to them at the end of the day, I suppose.'

'Oh, Liza, this is Cray,' said Rosie, then turning her eyes to Ferg.

Ferg reached out his hand to them. 'Ferg, and this is Sam.'

Sam piped up: 'It's only going to be for rich people.'

'Tourists,' Ferg said.

'Terrorists,' Liza snarled. 'Well, the poor darlings do need their weekend mansions, don't they?'

Cray didn't say anything, felt uncomfortable getting into the locals–tourists debate when he wasn't sure which category he and Rosie were considered to be in.

'It's depressing,' Liza said, trying to speak more gently. 'It feels out of our hands, despite these meetings and everything. It's one thing to chop up the land into squares so people can have their ocean views, but building shopping centres and hotels there – it's hideous.'

Everyone nodded at that. The hall was nearly empty.

Someone was unscrewing the microphone stand.

Sam said, 'But Mum, they won't do it if everyone's saying not to. Not if we're all saying no.'

'It'd be so nice if it worked that way, Sam,' Liza said.

Sam didn't say anything to that, but didn't look convinced either. Liza watched as he exchanged a smile with Rosie.

The microphone man began loudly stacking up the orange chairs.

'Looks like we're getting the wind-up,' said Rosie.

Liza wanted to say, 'Coming to the next one?' but wasn't sure, thought it would sound too much, and she didn't know why she was so keen anyway. She pulled her woolly cardigan on over her jumper.

Cray took a step back. 'Yeah, we'd better go and start warming up the Woody. Usually takes longer than the drive itself.'

The others laughed. Cold air gusted in through the doors.

'See you next Thursday, then, I guess,' Rosie said to them, to Liza.

'Yeah,' enthused Sam. 'We'll be here, won't we, Mum?'

All the way home Sam was thinking, thinking. He wanted to *do* something. He thought it sucked that everyone felt it was hopeless, wanted to show them that it wasn't, *it wasn't*. So he set about it when they got home, using his computer, of course. He imported graphics from the net and used the coolest fonts and printed his work out in super-wide landscape format for extra effect. Then he used some old textas he found jammed underneath his *Pocket Guide to Astronomy* and after about an hour he walked into the kitchen and pretended nothing unusual was going on as he stuck it on the fridge under the pineapple and *I Love Margaret River* magnets.

Liza and Ferg and Pip stared at him, stared at the fridge. When he stood back, they read:

DON'T JUST SIT THERE!

If you love our coastline help protect it.

Recreation Centre meetings every Thursday, 7.30 pm

Show your face or be in disgrace.

© This poster was designed by Sam Crowe for the Margaret River Coast Protection Society

Sam particularly liked the last couple of lines. He liked the new organisation he'd invented. Founding member: Sam Crowe. And his parents' faces when they were reading it. He walked out of the kitchen, cool as a snowdog. Tomorrow, he'd take it to school and ask to put it on the noticeboard. The librarian might let him put one up in the library, too.

44

Rosie slumped into the passenger seat of the Woody, smile slipping off, as they left the carpark.

'What's the matter?'

She didn't want to talk, she didn't know what she thought, she didn't know what she wanted to say.

'Rosie?' Cray turned on to the highway, rolled down the main street past the night-lit shops.

'Nothing, nothing, just ignore me. I'm being silly.' She wished she'd just kept the smile on, kept any loose inadequacies strapped down.

Cray had his suspicions about what this was. Rosie had a crazy habit of comparing herself to others with unhealthy frequency. If she liked someone – like Liza, say – she'd decide that she needed to be more like them. Cray anticipated a day or two of Rosie-reassuring. 'Rosie.'

She shook her head at the window. Just this non-discussion was making the whole thing bigger. She should have learned by now to keep the small things in a bit longer, fight them herself, see if they passed or grew.

'It's nothing! It was just a moment of, oh, I don't know ... just ...'

'What?'

'I just get sick of myself, that's all. I wish I wasn't ... I really like her – Liza. That's all. It's not a big deal – well, it wasn't a big deal – so just ignore me, alright? Please?'

Cray turned into Calgan Road. The forest was darkness either side.

She turned back to him. 'They were nice, weren't they?'

'Yeah.' Cray looked across at her. He tried not to be too

enthusiastic. 'Sam *should* be able to believe that if a community says "no", they get "no", because that's how a community works, because that's what's bloody right.'

Rosie wished she'd been thinking about that, rather than indulging in self-centredness. She leaned her head on Cray's arm. 'You're right.' The lights of the Kingswood cut a clear path ahead, threw yellow into the forest. Cray took his arm off the wheel, and curled it around her neck.

45

Rosie looked out at the whipped-up ocean and wondered if the house could cope with the wet buffeting, if its weatherboard planks would swell and split and give up.

She recognised a couple of stationwagons idling at the Edge Point carpark, passengers assessing surfability. If she went to the Greys Bay general store now – or anytime – she'd be served by the people who lived behind the shop in an unlikely brick extension, and she would wait alongside one of the store regulars, maybe Dave or Morgs, shaking a choc-milk languidly before wandering outside to sit in the weak sun, and try to warm like a lizard. The cold of the ocean stayed with you for hours after a surf in winter, Cray told her, it got into your bones and made your blood sluggish.

But she didn't go to the store, couldn't think of anything worse right now. She felt low. Probably just the weather, she thought, watching the wind chimes slap and twist and arc at each other on the balcony. Their first winter in Margies was nearly over, but it had seemed to last so much longer than winter in Perth.

She pressed in her folks' phone number, the soft squares of rubber giving way under her fingertip.

'Hey, Dad. You don't normally answer the phone.'

'Rosie! Your old Dad does surprising things every now and then.'

'I know, sorry. And you're not *that* old – not yet.'

'Jeez, thanks! Apparently seventy is when the rot really starts to set in. Anyway, enough! How're things with you?'

'Fine.' Rosie could never bring herself to say *Shit, horrible,*

I want to come home, and anyway, she wasn't even sure that that *was* how she felt. She didn't want to go home, she knew what that was like. 'The weather's a bit of a challenge at the moment,' she said.

'Get the heater going, then, love, and put an extra jumper on.' He relayed to her mum: 'She's feeling cold down there, dear.'

A muffled tutting came through, and Rosie heard them conferring, but her dad must've had his hand over the receiver, as she'd seen him do so many times before, because she couldn't make any of it out.

'Rosie,' he came back on the line rather loudly, 'Mum says to tell you to use a couple of door sausages to keep the draughts out.'

Rosie laughed out loud at that. Her oldies really were more like grandparents than parents. 'How is Mum, Dad?'

'She's fine. She wants to talk to you. She's telling me to hurry up. How's Cray?'

After a brief run-down, and before passing the phone over, her dad said, 'You guys must almost be considered locals down there, now. Your Mum and I think it's great, what you and Cray have done, Rosie, really – brave ...' There was a slight pause. 'Greys Bay's a beautiful place.'

Huh? *Cray*, not Ray? And *brave*?

'Oh ... thanks, Dad. I think you need to be here for a few generations before you're a local, but that's ...'

'Well, I won't be here in a few generations to tell you then.' He laughed gently.

'Oh, Dad!'

'Here's Mum. We'll see you soon, dear.'

Rosie glazed her way through the conversation with her mum, tried not to be distracted by what her dad had said. *You stay down there* ... To have it confirmed like that, out loud.

Even after she'd hung up she sat near the phone. Through the glass doors, the ocean had no patterns, no neat lines, no easy shape. It heaved and cut and crashed into the land.

46

Mike rolled the stuff around in his mouth, to check the consistency. He'd need a beer next to get the syrupy stuff off his teeth and tongue. After giving him his dose, Grant the surfing nurse completed the paperwork. A nurse he'd not seen before was restocking a trolley with vials and bottles and swabs and syringes, picking and choosing from the cabinets, unlocking the next and locking the last with the bunch of keys that jingled across her hip. Nice hip it was too, Mike thought, as he took note of those keys and the general contents of each cabinet. Those cabinets were like lolly counters at the deli after school, or the chemist you considered ramraiding in the dead of night.

He squinted at Grant. 'You sure this stuff isn't diluted?'

Grant looked up at Mike, bemused. 'Mike, don't be ridiculous. We're not your supplier. This is a hospital, remember.'

'Well, it tastes watered down, and I was having withdrawals at lunchtime from the last lot.' Mike heard the wheedling sounds of a spoilt five-year-old, or a paranoid user, in his voice.

'*Watered down!*' Grant nearly laughed.

Another nurse came in then. She looked older, like she was in charge. 'Sorry, couldn't help but overhearing. We'll have to up your dose then, won't we? Which means you'll have to come down all that way again, milligram by milligram, and each time you do that you're less likely ever to get off the stuff.'

Mike wanted to tell her to piss off; who was she, anyway?

'We *want* you to get better, Mike,' Grant said.

As she walked away he heard the older nurse say, 'My brother's still on it. Twenty years on methadone and still going strong.'

Mike walked over to the bottleshop. It was Margies' only drive-through, but you could wait there in your car as long as you liked, you'd still have to get out and get your booze from the shop. Sometimes they might carry a carton to your car boot if you were looking feeble.

Beer, vodka: which was cheaper, which could he get more drinks from? He concentrated on the alcohol because his mind was trying to stray to substances other than fluid. He even swung his eyes over the casks of moselle and *summer wine*. The idea that wine came from fruit was one he'd always struggled with. He'd never eaten fruit when he was a kid (nor as an adult, now he thought about it), despite the orchard. And yet he drank the stuff at every possible opportunity.

The orchard. Shit. Shit, the orchard. Mum. Pip. He was meant to have pruned ... Why was it taking him so long to get his shit together? He wasn't working – there hadn't exactly been a rush for his services since he'd moved down – so he had the time. But still he couldn't seem ...

After that he couldn't look at the wine. He bought the cheapest vodka and went back to his car, trying to ignore the neon sunset and the kookaburras, the odd carload of crazy punters driving home from the beach, salty and smiling, with kids piled, blue-lipped, in the back. And the trees, everywhere he looked, and definitely where he didn't, trees together like some feral family, surrounding him, closing in.

47

Even after telling Cray what she'd decided to do, it had taken Rosie a good while to summon up the courage to pay a visit to the editor of the local paper. The *Southern Way*'s office was an old weatherboard house in town, the editor's office the master bedroom.

'Well, we'd love to have you on board, Rosie, the problem is there's not a hell of a lot going on at the moment ...' He twirled his pen, looking at her, then gazed at one of the pieces of local art hanging on the wall. 'But ... the back page column needs someone – we call it Coffee Time.' He smiled apologetically. 'It's just a friendly weekly feature about a local identity, you know, a family who's been here for six generations, or the new apprentice at the permaculture centre, something like that, pretty gentle stuff. Jacqui gets sick of doing them every week, that's all, it'd be nice to give her a break ...'

Yeah, so you two can go for it hammer and tongs on your desk instead, Rosie thought, remembering what Liza had told her.

'Well, that sounds great,' she said, trying to ignore the image of him naked on his desk, bumcheeks squashing media releases. *Coffee Time. Possibly the pinnacle of my career.* 'I really appreciate the opportunity.'

Rosie felt vaguely sick about going back on the promise she'd made to herself.

'When do you need the copy by?'

After that, they shook hands, Rosie excelling at the grateful young person, and him playing the career mentor to a tee.

But a weekly feature, she thought. No muck-raking, no anonymous calls, no politics – council or office. And no Leighton tower.

Town was busy with people meeting friends, trucks hauling loads along the highway. She chucked her CV and folio on the passenger seat of the Woody and drove to Nurrabup, to the tiny salty cafe, where she knew she had a chance of being on her own with her thoughts.

When she drove up, Rosie saw the woman who ran the cafe, her hair wrapped up in a different piece of fabric today. She and a couple of seagulls were cleaning the tables outside.

There was no way around it; Rosie couldn't reverse out of the carpark now. She'd just have to get used to this, this total lack of anonymity. She realised now how much she missed that part of living in the city. Here, wherever people were, there was someone you knew. That was the way it worked. She'd just have to think about the *Southern Way* column later on, at home.

After the usual friendly preliminaries, the woman said, 'Have you been coming to the meetings?'

'It's great, isn't it? They're really keeping up the momentum.'

'We just can't let it happen,' the woman said. 'There's an energy about this place ... It's not like anywhere else I know.'

Rosie nodded vaguely, thinking: *'Energy', please, give me a break*. But she said, 'The rec centre's been packed, hasn't it? Though I doubt it's going to make any difference now – like you said, they've got it all planned. We're just delaying the inevitable, aren't we?'

'Well, yeah, I s'pose. And they're using the argument that the development will *contribute* to the town – services, jobs — so they're getting lots of support that way. I mean, if it was just out-and-out logging for woodchips or something they'd never have a chance. But they've made it sound ... good to a lot of people.'

They turned to look at the proposed site.

'God, it's unbelievable, isn't it,' Rosie said.

She and Cray had walked through there last week. There were hundreds of arum lilies starting to bloom, and peppermint trees swayed over the smooth white cups. The lilies were weeds down here, she knew, but she thought they were beautiful all the same. In the bush it was dark and cool. Rosie felt furious — was it too much to ask, to want? A place that was left just as it was? Where birds scooped in and out, animals scuttled low down and the wind sent waves through the bush, like a sheet being thrown over a bed. She shook her head. She couldn't think of anything good that could come out of ploughing it down. Nothing.

Rosie was glad she'd had to chat to the cafe owner, after all. It was good to talk to people. It wasn't what you said, or didn't say. It was more a matter of being part of something, she thought, of the human exchange.

The following week, Rosie dropped the copy on his desk. It was a good story, a lovely story. It had been a pleasure to listen to the eccentric old woman, her dancing eyes, the way she called her *Rosie dear*, voice wavery.

Eight hundred words later, and she had Coffee Time (that *name*!): the story of a woman who'd been born in Margaret River and had lived here ever since. It was a great way, Rosie thought, of getting to know a town that was at the same time open and closed to newcomers. A great way to neutralise the brain-deadening effect of working at the hotel, without having to give up the job altogether. (There *was* something in the pulling of a beer from a silvery wet tap that satisfied her immensely.) She still felt sick, though, when she thought about admitting it to Nat and Salt, to her folks; saying she'd gone back. Thank god for 329 kays.

On the way back to the house, Rosie dived into the nippy turquoise water at Hut's Beach. A few metres out she turned to face the shore, looked up to the top of the hill where you could just see their house and, sometimes, the shape of a man on the verandah, searching for patterns in the swell.

But today was too calm for swell. Rosie let her body sink through the shades of cold, and settled on the ocean floor.

48

At the meeting that evening, Rosie scanned the information being handed around about the Nurrabup development. She couldn't imagine anything the area was less suited to than the developers' original – and thankfully rejected – plan for a golf course. When council didn't approve it, the developers sold it back to the local bloke they'd purchased it from. So he'd already made a hefty profit from the stuff-up, but now of course he wanted more. Subdivision had been approved by council. Sketchings of a shopping centre and hotel had been accepted. RAID was trying to get anything they could now, height restrictions, buffer zones, anything to lessen the impact. Anything to stifle the arrogance of council.

'What about the sewage from the area, Mr Hanlen?' Someone was on his feet, notes in hand. 'It says in the plans that effluent from the estate will be pumped into a "ponding area", meaning it'll be left to seep into the sand – eventually the sea.'

People shifted in their seats, straightened up to hear the response. Heads nodded and shook, people murmured to themselves. Rosie didn't know the speaker but clearly he knew what he was talking about.

The guy continued. 'We know you reckon you've got this all wrapped up, Mr Hanlen, but if you think this community's gunna sit by and let you wreck it out there, you've got another think coming.'

Rosie's knees pushed her up. Kids and oldies were cheering, clapping, *hear-hear*ing. Plumbers, hippies, business people, surfers, waiters, farmers. Rosie grinned wildly. Mister Stokes – Bernie – and some of the kids he taught who'd come with their parents were crammed in at the back. Across the room, Liza and Ferg and Sam.

He was shouting now. 'We're the people of this town, Mr Hanlen,' – he looked around at the faces – 'and we have time. We'll stick this out as long as it takes.'

The whole room was on its feet. The hair on Rosie's arms went vertical. Cray had his whistle fingers jammed into his mouth. The stage microphones were useless.

49

Sam was finding it hard to wind down after the meeting. He glanced at his computer, its shut-down screen. He wasn't allowed to log on this late. He was meant to be getting ready for bed.

He thought about the situation at Lumptor while he rummaged about for his PJs. Last time he'd checked, the planet was hanging on. But Sam thought he might have found a loophole to help save the Lumptorians, if only there were some way he could let them know. He'd found a way of disarming Valstran's vapour-armour, he was almost certain. This was chemical warfare, after all. Valstran had no problem eliminating Lumptor's essences, preventing the respiration of its inhabitants, so why should Lumptor stick to the rules? As far as Sam was concerned, now was no time to be nice.

He peered out the window. It was a black night out there. Even the marri's outline had disappeared into the blackness.

As he pulled his jarmie top over his head Sam spotted his backpack dumped on the floor, and remembered that his lunch was still in there. Yuck. Festering sandwiches with slobbery tomato. He'd told Mum about not putting tomato in his sandwiches – it soaked into the bread and by lunchtime it was like eating an old sponge. Wet bread. Ugh. The thought of it made him bare his teeth. He took the lunchbox into the kitchen. He had a couple of notes Mum had to sign. Excursions. One to some local factory (thrilling), and the other to a surf carnival. Sports days were okay, at least you could take munchies and frozen cordial in your drink bottle and cheer for your team.

In the lounge, Ferg, Liza and Pip sat staring at the TV. No one was talking. Sam saw Dad get up and snap off the set.

Pip came to, then, with a little snore, tried to pretend she'd been awake all along.

'This is ridiculous,' said Ferg.

Liza was tired. Nothing anyone said would help, but Ferg looked at her like he wanted an answer.

'It's not the end of the world, Ferg! Yes, Mike was late and yes, Pip missed her doctor's appointment as a result. But I called the surgery to apologise and I don't think your mum's too worried about it, so let it go.'

'But it's like it's my fault now! Why am I feeling bad, for Christ's sake?'

'Probably because you're going on and on about it!'

Sam backed away to the kitchen so he could hear the rest in safety.

'For *Christ's* sake, Mum, go to bed if you're tired.'

Oh god. Poor Nan. After a pause, Sam heard her say, *Well goodnight then!*, and something about the Lord's name.

'Oh fuck!' Ferg pleaded with Liza.

Sam looked around the kitchen, at his old blue lunchbox. He'd lost the lid last year; they'd been playing frisbee with it at recess. Now it had an orange lid that didn't quite fit: the corner always popped off.

He had the notes in his hand.

Sam tucked the pages under the poking-up corner of his lunchbox lid, didn't breathe in while doing so lest the fetid sandwiches reached him, then ran down to his room. He closed the door behind him.

Home.

50

Sam was propped up in his bed, reading, when someone knocked very quietly. And, wrapped in his daggy old terry-towelling robe, his dad poked his head around the door.

'Sam,' he whispered.

He came over and sat on the edge of the bed. Sam put down his book and looked at his dad. Outside, the marri swayed, talked in night languages.

Sam waited for him to say something, to explain why he'd come in, was still waiting when his dad tried to chase away a salty bead straying down his cheek. Only thing was, he flicked it onto Sam. Sam didn't know what to do. His dad was ... well, he was crying, and not saying anything. Sam looked at Captain Kirk on the base of his lamp, as if he might tell them what to do.

Sam reached over and hugged him, as best he could. Squeezed his dad's humping shoulders.

51

From the cottage window, Mike could see the main house, with its golden-lit windows. He imagined Liza curled up on the couch next to his brother, both of them reading, while Sam dreamed of technologies yet invented and Pip nodded off in her chair.

He thought about the scars in the skin of his over-used arms, the gaping wounds in his head, his screwed-up head. Tree shadows leaned over the cottage, conferred among themselves. He thought of how he'd forgotten the doctor's appointment he'd promised to take Pip to that day. By the time he'd made it back to collect her it was too late. He was always too late. Too late for everything. He thought of the line of Liza's neck. The way her collarbone lifted her freckled coppery skin. Mike looked down at his grubby jeans and worn boots, at the way earth was jammed into the cracks in the boots' leather, ground into the creases where his toes bent with each step.

He was hungry. He scanned his inadequate food collection – tins of tomatoes, tinned corn and beans – and felt ashamed that he could not, at this stage in his life, look around at a good steak, fresh eggs and a loaf of bread, and maybe even the odd vegetable or two. He was sitting in the sag of an old single bed, and somewhere in the world was a woman he loved, who had once loved him, who had lain at night with her ear at his lips, listening to him, wanting his words, noticing the sliver of moon, its opaqueness, when life was clean, when he was clean, before he sullied it all with grubby need.

52

Sam's eyes shone with light reflected from the screen. He'd turned down the volume to zero, so he could hear anyone coming towards his room. He'd switched off his room light. If someone came, he'd cover the screen with his lever-arch file and launch himself into bed.

No one came. And that night Lumptor fell.

As he read, Sam felt spewy. He couldn't believe it. The planet was shrouded in grey gases concocted by Valstran's lab army.

He'd always thought it would be okay, all this time he'd been following the story; that the people of Lumptor would stumble across a solution – his solution! That Valstran would end up being their slave, or something. That the good guys would win.

But Lumptor was cyber-ash.

Sam concentrated. *That old good-guys-win-bad-guys-lose stuff is crap*, he thought reluctantly. Seppo schmaltz, his dad called it. Sam usually agreed with him, but ... well, he'd hoped the Lumptorians would crush Valstran into a pulp, after they'd tortured him, that is.

After a little while, after his Mac had made the whirring sounds of shutdown, Sam went to bed. At least tomorrow wasn't going to be a totally boring school day – they were going to the surfing carnival in the afternoon, and a couple of the guys from his class were competing. They were the same guys who always got picked for interschool sports, all-round legends.

The house was quiet, apart from someone moving about in the kitchen. Mike hadn't been around much in the last couple of days, and at dinner his dad had hardly said a thing.

Dejected, Sam pushed himself deep into his bedclothes, and drifted away to a dreamless night.

53

That morning, Sam flew out of the kitchen, bleary-eyed, barely having touched his toast. *Can't be late, Mum!*

That morning, Ferg felt dreadful. He'd been up so late, wandering, suffering in a way that is only possible to do at night. Eventually, he'd conked out on the sofa, pulling all Liza's cushions on top of himself to keep warm.

Leaning against the kitchen benchtop, he dropped two teabags into his huge mug, and flicked the switch on the kettle. And closed his eyes again.

That morning, Mike stood under the shower for a long time. He went through much of the bar of soap Liza had left in there and even cracked the shampoo. Once dry, his skin pulled inwards, pulled tight, as though even it was shocked by this new order. Then he sat on his bed again, unsure of what to do next.

That morning, when she got back from the school run, Liza peered into her crusty old gardening gloves, blew fiercely, then quickly pulled her face away in case a spider (redback, white-tipped, ordinary garden variety) should come bowling out. She was looking forward to a day of getting stuck into it, a productive day, hopefully, at the end of which she could look over the orchard and see her effort, feel her body's weariness, her skin beating from the sun.

That morning, Pip sat by the plum tree with a Joanna Trollope in her hands, looking over at Liza occasionally. She was more than a little unsettled by the goings-on around the place recently. You could use a knife, she thought unhappily. Ferg had hardly been at home and, when he was, he'd swear at the smallest things. He didn't talk to Liza, ignored the fact that she was cooking specially for him: lamb roast, cannelloni with ricotta, pear crumble. He stayed up late, staring furiously at the TV, and she heard him go to work at five-thirty most mornings. As soon as he'd left the house Pip would sneak into the kitchen for her first cup of tea. She'd been awake for an hour by then. Mike was a different kettle of fish, unpredictable, fickle. Especially, of course, when he'd got caught up in drugs and all sorts. They were grinding years for all of them. Jack took it so hard, tried so hard to pull Mike out of it. But it got messy, and Jack stopped talking to her about it altogether. Went quiet. And then he was dead. What would he have thought of this? What would he say to the son who pulled himself away from his family till they barely knew him? Whose marriage split up without any of them knowing there was even a problem? And to the other son, who bitterly went about his dead father's business, who loved his wife and his boy but found angry solace in his work? Pip looked at Liza, skin shining with heat. She was a loyal woman, Pip thought. She'd had some tough times, she could be difficult, but she wasn't going anywhere in all this. That, Pip and Jack had always known.

It was relationships, the quality of them, that mattered. That was all that mattered.

The long morning stretched ahead.

54

The classmates slopped with the ocean on neon boards, a huge waterbed that wouldn't settle. The sounds of the sea were in their ears. The carnival was a perfect chance to bring their passion into the school day, and they caught waves and watched for swell out the back, the odd jibe thrown over the shoulder just as they took off. Beneath their fingers were lumps of sand-freckled wax that their toes dug into when they crouched and stood up. Their wrinkled fingertips were a surfer's universal clock.

One of the girls was on a nice right when the earth swelled and burst on shore. She must have heard something – a cracking? a cry? – for she looked over to where her friends and teachers sat, but there was only a puff of white dust where they'd been, and she scanned the coast either side, in case she'd become disorientated, but there was nothing, no one. She turned back to the others, questioning.

55

The phone was ringing. Rosie, home from an afternoon shift at the hotel, heard it from the driveway as she pulled in. She heard it as she quickly crunched over the gravel from the car; as she tried to slot the key in the front door (*upside down!, c'mon*); as she came into the house.

No one was out there, despite the lines of swell coming in. Perfect conditions, she thought vaguely.

That phone call had a persistence about it. It rang and rang and the noise filled the house, and as Rosie finally reached it, and spoke, and heard, the ringing grew all around, grew to a colossal stillness, and then came a distant chorus of sirens bawling.

In town, someone ran to the row of three phone boxes outside the tourist bureau, while Commodore and LandCruiser and Kingswood engines shuddered into strange life. People stood in the middle of the street, as if awaiting an announcement, a car with a loudspeaker, *something*.

Silence settled heavily as limestone dust rose and hung, suspended over the beach, over that sheltered bay.

56

At the end of the afternoon, when the sky had the colours of orchard fruit in it, and Pip had gone inside to watch *The Price is Right*, Liza pulled a handful of new raspberries from protesting brambles, and walked down to the river. To hear its clean splashy sounds, to get close to Sam's spot (Sam hadn't been dropped home from school yet, she noticed, probably devising science fiction plots with Jarrad), and to just enjoy her own company, her own hard day, for a few moments. Ferg would be back from the trees in an hour or so.

At a narrow section in the river she slipped her way over rocks and branches to the thick natural forest of the other side, one of the few belts of original Margaret River forest remaining. The sun had already retracted from deep in there, and Liza felt the strength of the giants around her, as evening came down, a show about to begin.

Liza went right in, to feel the last of it, the last of that place on that day in September. She pushed through ferns and the thorny tentacles of bush creepers into the greying heart of the place. In the west, treetops scuffled with the wind.

If she'd been at the ocean, Liza would have seen it like the wind coming in from the horizon, turning the glassy water choppy and dark. Here, in the forest, she could hear the wind long before she could see it. It sheeted over the most distant trees, coming like a thundercloud on a blue day.

The sound of a big wind gaining across the green, coming towards her. A fire, of wind.

It came until she thought it couldn't be any bigger, that sound. Leaves and branches started up around Liza like crazed conductors, gathering force until, eyes down in fear, she pressed herself against the nearest trunk, some kind of shelter against the tree-spears crashing down around her. Widow-makers, Jack used to call them, she remembered now wildly. Foresters found pinned like ants to the ground, axe a few metres away.

It came heaving across the canopy, until Liza thought it couldn't come anymore. That sound, that wind. That breath.

Sudden energy invades the marri like a current. Its canopy swings and swipes, spraying leaves and conkers, hard nubs of its bloody sap, over the empty house. Then it stops, just like that.

Not far away, in the forest beside the river, a woman stands frozen beside a tree, her heart full of fear.

57

Liza ran. Ran and ran. At the bottom of the loose-stoned driveway, she bent double and sucked air across her stick-dry throat.

Behind her, across the river, the forest was still, as if nothing had happened just a few moments ago, as if a spiral of wind had never even tousled the leaves of the trees there, as if branches had not speared down around her amid a wind that gathered force like a cyclone.

As if this were the eye.

Liza peered through the bush at the highway, waiting for Jarrad's mum's car, or Ferg in the truck, or someone. Instead, she heard the guts of an urgent vehicle as it changed down for more speed up the long sloping hill past their place. It passed her like the movement of clouds in a storm sky.

A siren smudged past. The doctor's car. The volunteer SES truck, with all the guys in it.

Liza shrank back, turned to the farmhouse.

58

Rosie ran down the long hill towards the Edge Point carpark in lunging strides, sandals nearly flying off. Her breath came up at her in primitive sounds with each thump of her feet on the road.

Greeting her was the ocean's lapping rhythm. She leaned hard against the Koppers logs, scanned Hut's Beach below. Nothing. She looked for it, but couldn't see anything out of the ordinary. Just the limestone cliff walls and sand, and water. She headed down the steps, small birds swooping in front of her, saltbush reaching for her legs. Ten metres down, she saw a huddle of jumbled colours, people close together. And something in that view had changed – as if the sky itself could change – a whole part of the limestone cliff had collapsed on to the beach, given up, given itself up to the repeating water. A mass of cream rock lay heavy where the entrance to the local cave was.

Was.

Toy people were crawling on top of the pile, pulling the pieces away. Others were sitting further away, arms clutched about their knees.

A woman came scrambling up the impossible path, calling out to God. She made it to the top, to Rosie standing with nothing, no way of helping.

The measured wailing crept closer, it couldn't be far away now. Together they turned and looked over at the town, to the winding road over the tiny bridge, and waited.

59

He still had sight of the sea, cool-burning in him. But it had gone blue-black like the turning sky at night, just as the stars come over that impossible horizon. And the stars were here, he saw their clear brightness, their endless possibilities and promises and connections. A whole sky of stars, there were so many, everyone could have a whole skyful to themselves and there would still be plenty left for others, because the sky never ended, it had no edges, it was wider than anything comprehensible, wider than Sam and Margaret River and Western Australia, wider than your imagination, wider than existence itself.

Sam saw them, could almost reach out and touch them: the marri, the falcon and the fish, the river and the rockpools and sand dunes, the wind, and his family who moved among them all, took comfort from them, together, now, together in his perfect, dusty vision.

60

By the time Liza and Ferg got there, by the time Cray had driven past on the way home from work and seen the commotion, by the time the first news crew had arrived from the network in Colburn, most of what would happen had already happened.

A local bloke took his bulldozer out there, scooping up the slumped cliff that the town knew so well. This was where they walked with their kids after school, boards and towels and bathers in tow. Where the young ones stood wobbly on foamies before they graduated to fibreglass on the rivermouth, before they could even imagine the churning water of Edge Point, Surge Point. Where families parked their bums between swims, cooled by the shadow of the cave.

Which now buried some of them. Under a limey, dusty, suffocating mantle.

Eventually, floodlights, silvery-white and dazzling, were attached to the wreckage, glaring on the moving hardhats and orange boilersuits of the rescue crew.

Rosie and Cray were filling dozens of mugs and cups and bowls with tea in the carpark on a flimsy card table they'd set up, with a few other helpers. A woman spooned sugar into each mug. She put the sugarbowl down after a while, hands splayed on the tabletop, quietly gasping. Someone put an arm around her shoulder.

The generators below hammered. At least a hundred people were gathered in the carpark now; more paced the road, tried to avoid the fleet of ambulances, tried to keep upright. There was calling out, people were comforted, others faded. Cray moved about with the hot drinks. Rosie picked up two mugs and walked towards Liza and her husband.

She stood next to them until they noticed her. Liza was shuddering, but smiled quickly, bluely, when she saw Rosie. She took the mugs, passed one to Ferg, whispering to him. He didn't make eye contact with either of them. His eyes had the looseness of no focus, but he kept them turned to the cliff site, to the activity.

Rosie wanted to grab Liza's arm and ask, *Where's Sam?*, as if it mightn't be a possibility. As if he might be at home, or at a friend's place, or somewhere else. As it was, it was difficult to tell whether people were there for their own or for others; if their oldest friend's husband had been found, dusty and misshapen, among the rocks, and ferried to a sirenless ambulance, or if they were waiting to see the face, the favourite jacket, the honey hair of someone who hadn't come home yet.

The tonelessness of Ferg's face was Rosie's answer.

She turned her head back to the hill of houses and bush behind them, the mixture of fibro shacks and holiday homes, wooden cottages and oddly designed mansions, each empty, evening verandahs unattended, all with their lights on and front doors swinging open.

'I didn't sign the letter from the school,' Liza said suddenly. 'I found it in the kitchen this afternoon, so Sam can't be here. We didn't sign it—we didn't give our permission. He isn't here. He'll be with Jarrad.' She clicked her tongue, turned to Rosie. 'Those two, you know.'

Around them, people turned to and away.

Rosie wanted to reach out to Liza and unfold her and bellow. She wanted it to be day and she wanted to see the ocean, *see* it, lay her eyes on it, rather than be subjected to this, its blackening, oblivious rhythm.

61

A stenographer's notebook appeared next to Rosie's elbow.

'I didn't know you were here too ... it's Rose, isn't it?'

She peered at the woman. 'Rosie. Sorry, who are –'

'Katrina King from Channel Six. When did you get here? We arrived half an hour ago, we had to charter a flight to Brenn Head.'

'Oh, no, no, I'm ...' She looked at Liza and Ferg apologetically. 'Let's go over here, these people aren't –'

'You know them? Is someone they know down there?'

Rosie steadied. She hoped that by lowering her voice Katrina would drop her own a few decibels. 'Everyone knows everyone down there, actually. It's not just their children, it's their friends' kids ... it's –'

Katrina King flipped open her notebook.

'No, no, I'm sorry, I'm just talking to you as ...'

Katrina looked up. 'Aren't you reporting this?'

Rosie felt a cold sweat break out. People might think she and Katrina were colleagues. 'No. No, I'm not reporting it. I live here now.'

Rosie hadn't even thought about the *Southern Way* until then.

There were enough reporters here, she knew, enough reports being filed, enough being phoned through to the jaws of newsrooms. The world knew what was going on (it had already been given a name: The Greys Bay Cliff Collapse), and the local people certainly knew what they needed to know. That their loved ones were buried where they'd sat watching an inter-school surfing carnival (just hours ago, sifting sand through their toes); that their oldest friends were grappling through the rubble on their behalf, trying desperately to find a warm limb somewhere, trying impossibly to keep a clear head as a mate's son was found.

Rosie looked at Katrina and said, 'I know you're here to report, but, look, take it easy on these people.' She leaned in slightly to her, and Katrina met her confidence like a magnet. 'They can hardly face each other right now, let alone outsiders.'

Katrina nodded, though looked as if she still needed some convincing. Rosie saw with relief that most of the reporters were talking to local police and SES guys rather than to families direct.

Katrina's eyes scanned the clusters of people.

Rosie moved away from her. She went back to the edge, leaned out again over the Koppers logs to see what headway had been made, what boulders pulled, but she knew from the silent work going on down there that no one else had been found.

Lit up, the red and white television helicopter came around the headland. It blew the tops off waves as it cut a path across Surge Point towards the tiny emergency colours of the rescuers.

There was a quietness down on the sand, as boulders were delicately shifted and special maps and local information studied under torches. A muffled voice had been heard, by two or three of them. The maps fluttered as volunteers crowded around the SES leader. A *voice*, someone said.

Members of the crew began to look up, hair blowing. Water came up at them, slapping the sand and limestone harder and higher. A television crew roared above them, black eye of a camera aiming down. Above them, in the carpark, families watched the scene, pressing hands to their ears.

A voice.

Sand stung the rescuers' skin. Loudness filled their ears and every crevice of limestone remaining. Hopelessly, they waved, pointed, directed, ordered, prayed, begged that chopper to turn away.

Some of the onlookers openly seethed into the night, promising retribution. Others bloated with fear. Rosie tried to hide, collecting mugs, filling them, ferrying hot water from the general store in saucepans, buckets. A woman laid her hand on Rosie's arm. Katrina walked through the glarily lit crowd. One of the dads spat at her feet.

62

In the middle of that dark night Cray and Rosie walked up the steep hill, shushed by the grey shapes of bushes, to their house.

Every time Rosie started to say something about it, she'd think of something else that had to be said, something else to be worried about. Cray would look up, ready to listen, and she'd shake her head, unable to begin all that needed to be begun.

Not many others were still waiting when Liza and Ferg were approached by the police officer, Ferg's old mate from way back. Jesus, they'd gone to school together, Ferg had always given him shit about being the town copper, the Law Enforcer of Margaret River. It used to make Ferg chuckle, given the stuff they'd got up to as kids.

Now, their kids were the same age. And Ferg thought he was going to crack like something dropped when he saw his mate, the town copper, coming over with that steeled face. As the head copper he'd been doing this all night, Ferg had seen him, going to people. He looked around. There was just him and Liza left. And, slumped against the fading duco of the Sunbird, Mike was just behind them.

1

Mike stirred the plunger of coffee. Ground beans swirled, sucked down into the vortex. The spoon made an unlikely cheery sound against the glass. In the lounge, there were pauses strung together without any talk, the fullest silences air could hold. Mike put the pot down on the low table in front of them. Bright colours, a comic of Sam's, loudly caught his eye. He wondered, for a horrible moment, if he should move it, take it away. He looked at the counsellor, a middle-aged local woman who had driven from house to house to house since the collapse, had sat among terrible silences for days. How would hiding Sam's stuff help? Mike averted his eyes, his mind, left the comic where Sam had chucked it.

He pushed the flyscreen door out into the cool wind. Breathed. He wasn't thinking about it anymore, he kept it that distance from him – there but not there. A bird trying to land, unable to find a safe spot. He had to check the trees, he thought. The Tassies.

That bird hovered close when he found himself driving Ferg's ute between the blue rows. The last time he was in these trees he'd almost lost it. It couldn't get worse than this, he'd thought at the time; he'd finally made it to the sludge on the bottom.

He'd thought that once or twice before, he remembered now. But things truly couldn't be worse than this. Somehow, the kind of anger Mike had felt that night had drained away. All those years. He didn't have the energy anymore.

He changed gears, coasted through the rest of the rows. Didn't miss a one. Up and down, down and up like snakes and ladders, in his brother's ute. Pruning wayward branches, fixing fences, repairing the nets. His job for now.

In town, people cried when they came across each other in the supermarket. Kids and adults flocked to the surf shop, to the local schools, to lay flowers at their closed doors, to talk to people they loved, who loved them, to say things they couldn't – hadn't – said before. Families stuck together, went out together, crunched along the beach together, huddled together. Kept each other within reach. People cried at the oddest times, and everyone came to know there was nothing odd at all about this. People punished themselves for being able to carry on.

The emergency crews dealt with their own traumas. The twenty-year-old who pulled his father's body from the layers, and then climbed the path to tell his mum. The guy who reached his hand into a small hole in the rock pile and felt another grasp around it. He didn't go back to being the same man. She never left his head, that schoolgirl, who rasped her way out of the darkest place she would ever find herself; her mother's grey body a metre away. No one knew what to say to her father in the weeks following, just hugged the little girl till tears squeezed out of the corners of her miraculous eyes.

In Margaret River, in Greys Bay, nine people – five adults and four kids – would never come home from that surf carnival, from that cave, from that beach.

2

Hotels and B&Bs filled up with reporters and cameramen. TV stations televised special bulletins showcasing the updates of roving reporters, SES leaders, geologists, the guy who drove the bulldozer. Those interviewed spoke in unfinished sentences. Town spokespeople entered the spotlight in an attempt to shield the families, but still there were glimpses of broken husbands, parents, and children who understood something dark and lasting.

The site was cordoned off with orange flags. You couldn't recognise that bit of coast anymore; the rocks had changed its shape forever.

No one surfed out at Edge or Surge points.

Families went back to the carpark and leaned into the wind. Climbed gingerly down the path, a friend either side. They washed their faces in Hut's water, cupped it in their hands, hoping there might be something left to touch, to keep; something left.

On the day of the memorial service, the people of the town gathered in the carpark, overlooking the water, the beach, the endless limestone coast. Politicians came in suits and reporters came with back-up reporters.

Under the ultramarine sky that spring morning, a halo of kids, dads, daughters, sons, brothers, mates, floated out on the water, surfboards keeping them up. Cray went out too, swung his arms over and over into the water, pulling himself further out, through the green, the green-blue, the blue. The water breathed like a lung, moving them with it, and their circle widened a little, came in a little with every breath. A school of small silver fish darted in unison across the circle, slipping sideways from the shadows of the boards. The sharpness of the water caught between wetsuits and skin like cold comfort. They held hands, that human wreath, just beyond where the waves tumbled and crashed onto the shore.

3

A special church service was held after the beach ceremony. As people hugged each other and leaned against cars, friends, Ferg knew he just couldn't go home.

The parents of the children who had died stood together. Locals, old friends. He couldn't bear to go over there, to say their children's names, to hear Sam's, to be consoled. To utter a word, a sound. He didn't have it in him.

Home. On his own with Liza, and Pip and Mike, and the trees, and the marri, and the terrible silence. Liza, who stood next to him now, barely there.

Liza hung at the edge of the carpark next to Ferg with her back to the beach. Mike walked over slowly with Pip, his hand close to her elbow.

'I'll bring the car over. You guys stay here,' Mike said, and made towards the Sunbird.

'Home?' Liza spoke to no one in particular.

No, Ferg thought, *anywhere but there.*

'Aren't we going to the church service?' Pip said.

'Church service?' Liza turned to Ferg. 'We're not going to that ...' She looked confused. 'Are we?'

'Well, yes, I thought so,' Ferg mumbled.

'A *church* service, Ferg.'

He was quiet. Pip took a few steps away and pretended to rummage about in her bag for a tissue. Other people moved away from them. 'It might help,' he said.

'Help what?'

'I don't want to go home.'

'Help Sam? Will it help Sam?'

'Don't, Liza. Please.'

'Church isn't going to help us, Ferg! Nothing's going to help us.' She stared at him. She wasn't even close to crying. She hadn't made it to believing yet. 'We're fucked, Fergus! I don't know about you, but that's *it* as far as I'm concerned. I'm not trying anymore. *No more!*'

Mike's car crawled up. He crunched up the handbrake, stayed sitting in the car.

Ferg stood in the middle of the carpark, his hands swinging by empty pockets, the saltbush brushing next to him like steel wool.

'Don't, Liza, not here ...'

'Off you go to church, Ferg. Go and listen to some guy trying to explain it all away, as if Sam's not really—' She swung around, to the white rubble and orange flags, her voice stolen by the wind.

4

No one in Margaret River or Greys Bay rang in sick at work; no one was at work. Businesses were closed, some for weeks. Workmates didn't need an explanation.

After a few days, Cray went to the shaping shed, but couldn't imagine he'd actually work. Each time you saw someone you hadn't seen since the cliff collapse you'd have to go through it all again. Cray looked at the blank he'd been shaping on the day of the collapse. It was as if time had stopped since then, and all of a sudden he felt renewed energy to get back to it, to fire up the planer, pull his goggles on, and get back to normal.

Rosie wasn't going back to journalism ever, she had told him. The *Southern Way* editor had rung her to see if she'd do another Coffee Time column, but she thought it was just a ploy to get her in the office to report on the cliff collapse. She wasn't taking any risks. She loathed the whole business. Anyway, who would want to have a friendly chat for Coffee Time now? Who could muster the energy to look back over their lives and see how they'd become who they were, when one of their grandchildren might have just had the last breath pushed out of them? Rosie couldn't see herself writing feel-good features for the local rag when there were obituaries on the previous page.

Cray said it might help, hope was a motivator, it gave people a meaning, a reason. 'That's why I'm gunna make boards till they come out of my ears,' he told her, 'boards for every bloody man, woman and grommie out there, so they can get in the water, immerse themselves in it.'

'Bollocks,' Rosie said. 'How could it, Cray? How could that make things better?'

Cray imagined swimming through the aqua, watching the rolling water pass above him while he waited on the seabed, seeing the midday light piercing the moving skin of the ocean. At different times of the day, the light designed a different ocean. Somehow the water – just being in it – made you new again.

'Come out then,' Cray said. 'For a surf. See for yourself.'

Rosie rolled her eyes at him. 'But the reef ... the dumpings! And I don't have a board –'

'You can use mine.'

'I'm not a strong enough swimmer.'

'Bollocks to *that*,' he said. 'You know, Rosie, you don't want to let this place get to you, now, do you?'

5

Liza hung out the washing, though she really couldn't care less whether their shirts and towels got dry or went mouldy. Hanging them out was something to do. Like a robot needs something to do, because that's what a robot does. She could do that, Liza felt. Sit there all day, have no thoughts, no needs, just be the shell of her body sitting in a chair. She couldn't even think about her boy without feeling like she was going to black out. It wasn't real, was it, this? That was what she kept thinking. But if it was, it was her fault. Everything was her fault. She hadn't loved him enough, hadn't talked to him or listened to him enough, hadn't made his favourite sandwiches enough. (What *was* that? Why on earth hadn't she made him cheese and gherkin sandwiches every day? What had she gained by denying him those? It was just so stupid.) She gave in to these thoughts; someone to blame – herself – something to feel angry about – her mistakes – anything but the actual sadness. Pure sadness, sadness that filled her and reached right out of her; for her little man, for the world, for the life she had to continue making her way through, for *life*.

Sam.

There was nothing else she could add, to his life or hers. To this.

Mike walked around the house. Through the house. It was empty, though they were there. They were in their rooms, in the garden, among the gums, hiding from thoughts of Sam, expected sounds of Sam, his feet up and down the corridor, his computer, his mutterings to himself. How could absence feel like something? Mike had had to force himself to come into the house, after. It was crossing a threshold into terrible territory, and he'd realised that there was no changing this, that there was absolutely nothing that could be done.

Mike knew what they had to do. It was the one thing he'd learned from getting off the smack. Go for tiny changes, over lots of time. Time. He knew it would dull, eventually, with time, this pain. It wouldn't end, he knew that, too. But he didn't want it to, wanted to keep the pain, it was a way of showing respect for Sam. Mike felt he should feel like this every day, because Sam couldn't feel it, because Mike had wasted most of his chances over three times as long as Sam had had, and because this, *this* was life.

Pip remembered, though she did not want to, Jack's death. The shock of it, even though they'd known it was coming. The sudden arrival of Pip's remaining life alone, without him.

Pip felt familiar pain now; couldn't fathom how she was here again so soon. She looked about her room, at the life she'd made after life with Jack. A tiny life, really, cocooned in someone else's world like a child. And Sam. The family's child. The one they all moved around, turned around as he grew, oblivious to their focus. The centre of this old place. This place, Pip thought, that seemed to age alongside her, year by year, new cracks revealed with each passing spell.

And Fergus craved his son. His body yearned for him, a physical beckoning. The sound of his computer starting up behind his bedroom door – that steady industriousness of his. The statistics and definitions he'd proffer at the dinner table. The way he shadowed Ferg around the farm, just when Ferg needed him, somehow, offering to help. The smell of his hair, how smooth his skin was, the way his body was developing with each year, growing, hardening up. His hand, reaching out for Ferg's.

In his mind, Ferg's life was a murky pool, stirred up by mistakes and pain and history. Sam was a white-bellied fish slipping through it, turning in the sunlight to share a glint of silvery skin just when you thought he was gone, just when you thought the murky swirls had sucked him away for good.

6

Water seeped in at the neckline of Rosie's wetsuit – because it was Cray's, and therefore completely the wrong shape. She pushed herself from the board and held it by the rails as a little peeler came through from Hut's. Small, easy waves, said Cray. It's where everyone learns.

The membrane of water against her skin warmed gently with the sun. Still, she could imagine why surfers wee'd in their suits, particularly in winter seas. Rosie looked over at Cray, in his turquoise and yellow steamer.

'Beautiful wettie,' she called over the whitewater, grinning.

Cray nodded back, saying 'Watch out!' just as a wave broke on her, forcing her back about fifteen metres. Rosie paddled forward again, thanked him for the early warning. Her shoulders ached badly, and she had to fight the desire to hang her arms down into the cool water. She was sure there'd be white pointers circling below.

The waves did look pretty small, as far as Rosie could tell. She sat precariously on her board, parallel with Cray, looking out at water, sun, sky, waiting for whatever sign you waited for out here in the middle of the ocean. Now that she was *in* the water, she had no idea how Cray had picked this very spot – it looked all the same to her. (Rosie reminded herself, grinning as she thought it: a lot of research had been done, a lot of fieldwork.) Cray relaxed on his board, gazing at the horizon. Rosie looked down, wondering if there were any fish (or sharks), and the slight movement tipped her sideways into the blue. Coming up for air and composure, she looked at how Cray was sitting on his board and climbed back on. This time she tipped forward, the board shooting out behind her. When she came back up, Cray had turned to face the houses of Greys Bay.

He was paddling smoothly and, with a final kick of his feet, hoisted himself up. One smooth action. He faced the sky again and, knees soft, slid across the face of the wave, another world beneath and ahead of him. Rosie saw him disappear as the force of the water moved him south, towards the protective arm of the bay.

Rosie looked back and saw a hump of water moving towards her. She did what she'd seen hundreds of others do, but much more awkwardly: she spun her board around to face the land, and windmilled her arms through the cold. Rosie felt something pushing behind her, and hung on tight. Cray was laughing, and called out, 'Push up on your arms!', but Rosie just let the wave propel her closer to shore, and she was surprised by the force of it, she was really moving! Adrenalin prickled through her system and she grinned stupidly, even though she hadn't even got up on her knees.

In the white foam (very much like the creamy head of a good beer), Rosie pushed herself off the board and let the fizzy water buzz over her. She gathered the legrope and pointed the board back to the horizon, where Cray's shape bobbed, and paddled out again.

Rosie made a mental note not to let herself come in too close to shore next time, because the paddle back out was so far and so tiring.

After enthusing to Cray (it was like a natural rollercoaster, a rush, and free!) Rosie paddled into the next wave. As the water lifted itself behind her, Rosie's board nosedived and sent her into the impact zone, where she was drilled into the sand headfirst.

She came up, eventually. She had water up her nose and her eyes were stinging. She looked out and knew she'd lost her courage. For the day, anyway. Waving to Cray to stay out, Rosie turned to shore and guided the board, fingertips on lumps of wax, over the fizzing water.

Afterwards, Cray got Rosie to admit that it could be addictive. Certainly she knew she felt different for having been in the cold water that long. Hypothermic, she suggested. She took back the bollocks thing.

'Very generous.'

'Let's have something to eat.' She was feeling a little blue around the lips.

Cray sliced bread thick for toast. He filled the kettle and put a smoky brew of leaves into their small pot. Perfect.

Rosie wished she could surf. She hated to say it, but she wanted that almost spiritual bond with the water. It was something you could always fall back on, even when things made no sense or had no reason, you could always swim out towards the sky, and turn again to the land, that layered mound of sand and rocks and soil and time, the water between them, the sky and the land, keeping you up, keeping you moving.

7

Liza wanted Ferg out of the room. Seeing him reminded her of everything. She didn't know what to say to him. He looked like an old man. Liza was punishing him, she knew that. He knew that. That made her feel sick with anger. Stop it, she told herself. Reach out to him, look at him. He's broken, he needs you. He needs you to need him. Liza cried at that. *That* she could cry at; that was about her. Oh, she was weary. Look what she had become.

Liza felt dry, all the time, despite the tears she managed to shed, which was only when she was alone. Dry, like a constant hangover, her body harsh inside, not smooth or fluid. Dry. Like a fucking desert.

Ferg was trying to get her attention, was lingering.

'Want some lunch?'

Don't talk. Don't make anything normal. Lunch? *Lunch*? Liza didn't look at him, but managed, 'No thanks.'

'Lize, you've gotta eat.'

'No I don't.'

He looked at her for a few moments before leaving the room.

Liza wanted to smash something.

Ferg knew what she was doing, knew she couldn't stop herself. She'd done this before, years before, when she'd wanted to get pregnant again, and he'd felt it wasn't the right time between them, him and Liza. Ferg had wanted to wait until things were better, easier for them. She'd gone silent for weeks then, went into herself, pretended he didn't exist. Pushed him away, so far away he thought there was no way back in, back to her. This reminded him of then. This would go on and on until he broke it, until he broke through to her.

He didn't need this. He was grieving too. Jesus, he was.

8

Pip stuck the fork into the soil. The crusty top came away in plates, and she jammed the fork in again and twisted. *Bend your knees, old girl, you can't afford any problems now.*

A holiday, that's what she'd suggested to Ferg and Liza. Somewhere warm, tropical. Somewhere completely different from Margaret River. She and Mike would look after the trees. But Liza said no straight away, looked at Pip with those eyes, which meant, *Don't speak of it again.* Later, Ferg came in to explain, but Pip stopped him. She didn't take it personally. This thing had purged her of that.

Pip had rediscovered gardening since ... Since. All those afternoons, she thought disgustedly, lying on the bed watching *Days of Our Lives*. If she'd known she could still get down and delve around in the garden, if she'd remembered what it felt like to scrub black earth from her fingernails and feel the effort in her arms the next day! In the early days it had been one of her favourite pastimes, particularly after the orchard had been planted; something outside the house to get stuck into. Something outside herself.

She cooked regularly now, too. She tied the apron on and relearned her favourite recipes, ones she'd not used since Jack died. Though it was all she could do to get Ferg and Liza to sit at the table. Liza could hardly bring herself to go into the kitchen. Pip filled the silence with the beating of eggs, the slam of the oven door. Some days she only got up for the instinct to cook for them.

She moved over to a cluster of nightshade, pulled it up by the roots, a tiny eruption in the earth's crust. Pip stood, soil falling from her gloves. Sam should have seen his grandmother like this, she thought, not plonked in front of the set. *Sam.*

Further over, at the northern end of the orchard, the fig tree's bright green leaves scuffled newly, noisily announcing their season. Maybe it was too soon for a holiday, anyway. Maybe Liza imagined the two of them in a starchy hotel room on the other side of the country and the thought only magnified the strangeness of everything, the loss, their suddenly shapeless lives. Perhaps Margaret River was the best place for them to be, thought Pip. The place made sense to them. There wasn't much sense left in anything else.

9

Rosie had wanted to go to see Liza and Ferg, but had been avoiding it. She wanted to offer something, some strength, some small measure of companionship through this, though she knew those things would change nothing, that they were only words and feelings passing between people; a few moments in one day.

She didn't want to ring beforehand – what would she say? Everything sounded either too intense or glib. Instead, Rosie put a few things in a bag and slung it into the Woody.

She took the smooth snaking road down the hill, craning out at the surf. She knew she'd never know the ocean like Cray did, like the others knew it, but she longed to learn what she could. If you lived here, she'd decided, and you weren't interested in the water – if you didn't try to involve yourself in it somehow, even in some small way, like checking out the swell as you drove past, or trying to recognise the figures looking out at the horizon, their backs to the land – if you didn't do that, you were only keeping it at a distance from you. You were using the ocean as some kind of buffer between you and what you didn't understand, what you didn't want to understand.

So Rosie drove through town at the surf speed of twenty kays an hour, getting a glimpse of whatever it was out there that drew them all like a gentle rip, and when the view became too distant and glittery, she turned back to the road and concentrated on Liza and Ferg, and Sam.

In the last week Liza had relented on her anger, mainly because she couldn't summon it anymore. And because she finally recognised Ferg's distress. She'd seen him in the bathroom one morning, razor in hand, slack against the basin. She saw him come out again, still unshaven. Liza felt something go in her then, and had reached for his hand as he walked past. He'd looked at her, surprised, and Liza knew that they needed each other – Christ, now more than they ever had, ever would. They needed each other as Liza and Ferg, and as Sam's parents; they needed each other as the two young people who'd come together those years back, grinning embarrassedly and tenderly and dying to tumble into bed together, finding any opportunity. How they'd changed, she thought sadly. How very different they were now.

She was on her own, lying in an old deckchair in the garden, when Rosie arrived. The house was behind Liza, it was wide and open and Rosie could see down the corridor, could see the suggestions of rooms, but knew the doors to those rooms would be closed against emptiness.

Liza didn't get up, and she didn't look surprised to see Rosie, just said, 'Thanks for coming. There's a chair ...' and pointed to one on the verandah.

Rosie carried it over and sat down facing the garden. They both sat together and looked into the garden for some time. Rosie didn't want to start a conversation, though it would hardly be that, she thought, and instead she reached hesitantly for her bag. From it she took a small drawstring bag of sand and shells she'd collected from Hut's. She'd made the little cloth bag by hand the night before, and fingered it now, listening to the sounds the shells made as she turned it over and over in her hand.

'Oh, is that from ...'

Rosie nodded, and caught Liza's eyes for the first time.

'I hope it's okay,' she said, taking a breath. 'If you don't want it I understand.'

Liza looked at the bag without touching it, didn't say anything.

'Ferg would like it,' she said finally, and looked over at Rosie, as if to reassure her. 'He'd like it,' she nodded. 'Thanks.'

There was a pause before Liza pointed behind Mrs Perry's, at the sudden wall of green rearing up behind her house, and said, almost as if she were confessing something, as if she'd been saving up the memory for this, for now, for some time, 'I was in there when it happened; I was in the forest. There was a terrible windstorm, a terrible *churning* in the sky.' She stopped for a moment, surprised. Took a breath, made herself continue. 'By the time I came out, I knew there was something ... happening.'

Rosie stayed silent. She waited for Liza to go on.

Liza kept her eyes on the green, kept the words coming. 'I was so scared. I stood close to the trunk of a huge old tree. It's strange, no one else has mentioned it, that blow, as if maybe it didn't happen anywhere else. I must have been the only one in that bit of forest that day. Imagine Sam,' – she turned her face to Rosie, stricken, and caught on her words – 'how scared ...'

Liza's hand reached for Rosie's, and Rosie tried not to but cried as Liza wept, choking, sitting in her chair. Rosie looked at the hand in her own, and wondered how she had ended up here, in this garden, with Liza Crowe, and how it was still so new but somehow it wasn't; it felt normal, as normal as anything could feel. Then she took Liza's hand with both of her own and leaned forward, as if to say something, and waited as Ferg came over to the sound of Liza breaking, finally, and they sat together, in the garden, gathered round the small bag of sand and shells and what might have been the essence of their boy, some part, some spark of him, in the centre, in their centre, as it always would be.

10

Liza stayed in the garden after everyone had gone. She felt nearly still inside, for the first time in a long time. Beside her, the marri, too, was calm. It ticked and scratched with shifts in the wind. When the wind grew to anything more than a breeze, Liza's heart stumbled with the leaves that came down, until it lessened, softened, abated.

The marri was solid, but it was also vulnerable to that wind, to its every fluctuation, its every breath, its vacuums, its silences. It received whatever the days and nights brought.

Liza felt like a piece of something in the wind; as if the wind of that day had picked her up, caught her. She felt like a creature that had been shunted and spun into new surroundings, new conditions, a new existence. There was only so much that could be controlled, Liza told herself; after that you had to find other ways to get through.

Liza stayed a long time in the garden, until the sun retracted to another place and darkness lowered itself like usual, like sleep.

After that came the next day. The next day, and the day after that. With the usual sun, wind, swell, but days with gaps, with gaping holes like when you walked from old-growth into clearfelled forest, into that stick-dry, sandy wasteland left.

The sun glared through those holes. Nights were one big gap. Liza went outside most evenings, waiting for the stars to come out, and would try to remember what Sam had told her about constellations and galaxies. About shooting stars and Jupiter's moons. Sometimes the marri creaked and murmured and hissed so much she turned to it, thinking it could tell her something, that it would, somehow, let her know.

Mike would come out with his pouch of tobacco and sit with her sometimes. He never talked, just sat and rolled a crinkly cigarette. Liza would take the pouch and roll herself one, too. Her fingers shook as she rolled the paper around the brown threads of tobacco. Mike never commented on this; it made every sense in the world to him.

He had taken over the tree work from Ferg for the time being, taking the truck out and preparing areas for the next planting.

Liza and Ferg were glad Mike was with them, for that reason alone, but they didn't know how Mike was travelling with it, with the giving and helping and being around—*for once*, Ferg thought, but the bitterness in him had ebbed. Some days Mike's was the only face he could bring himself to look at.

Ferg was coping better than she was, Liza knew that. He went to counselling and tried to sort it out in his own mind, he let himself cry and talk, gave himself a break from work. Ferg tried to coax her, to help her, and Liza appreciated that, loved him for it, but she just couldn't do too much of it yet. She still couldn't talk about it much, but didn't think she'd ever be able to, really. When she managed to say things about it, out loud, she felt like an actor saying someone else's words. But Liza thought about Sam all the time, every minute, and talked to him, silently, every day. And while she couldn't bring herself to go into Sam's room, she sometimes heard Ferg go in, heard the computer start up with its familiar sound.

11

Mike only had another eight weeks on the methadone before he was on his own. He didn't tell Liza and Ferg, but Grant the surfing nurse was really pleased about it, said that he'd only treated two others who'd actually got off the program. Mike didn't tell him he'd had a few goes before this one, didn't want to ruin a good story. And hearing it made him feel pretty good, in a sad sort of way. Maybe a beer to celebrate his screwy victory.

At the pub, he soaked up the condensation from his glass with a Guinness coaster, and tore another into small bits.

He'd never got around to installing the latest version of Netscape on Sam's Mac; he'd always been too busy, too preoccupied with his own crap. It was all the kid wanted of him, and he'd never delivered. The shame was like a rash that he couldn't get rid of. He'd never forgive himself.

There were a couple of old blokes at the bar. He wondered how long they'd been resting up against that bar at the end of the day, how long they'd been coming. Did they have anyone waiting for them at home, or just a silent, empty house? How lucky he was, Mike thought, that Ferg and Liza and Pip had made room for him at the farm, had welcomed him back. He could have been one of these guys without them.

Mike was sweating from the trek through the bush.

Catching his breath, he crouched uncomfortably in front of the stone. A gang of twenty-eights pulled in at the local marri hangout, squawking flashily to each other.

Jack Garnet Crowe
1903–1987
Loving husband of Pip,
father of Fergus and Michael

It was too late, he knew that. Too late for Jack, and for him.

Mike yanked out a tuft of grass now, spraying dark-smelling soil over his father's plaque. The twenty-eights rose as a crowd and then settled again, bending the bough under their weight. He brushed the dark earth back, pressed it back into the ground where it belonged.

He followed the track further down after that, right down to the river, the way Sam used to go. Margaret River. All that water, going in the same direction, day after day, century after century. Lifetime after lifetime.

It took him a few hours, ducking and jumping and crawling, but he followed the path to the mouth of the river. In winter, the river would once again flow right across the sand here into the ocean, and course into adjoining oceans, and rivers, and clouds, and bellies, and soil.

Me and Mum, Mike thought. *We've gotta get it together and make a plan. Otherwise Ferg and Lize, they're gunna implode. And that can't happen. For Sam's sake, I'm not letting that happen. We're the last ones, me and Mum, the only ones who can bring them through this.*

In the wind, near where the river and the ocean met, Mike felt his bones rub together like sticks for a fire. He heard the sea strike the land over and over. He heard the twigs of shrubs play rough-and-tumble with the wind.

12

Rosie went over the back of the Greys Bay hill. A crowd of terns spun on her approach, a golden kite flew into the weather above a dune, hovering, the occasional pull of its wings keeping it there. Rosie was alone on that beach, and Cray was in the house on the back of that hill – probably with his feet up on the wooden balcony. Around her was the circle that the water made with the land, the sky, with Greys Bay.

With the sky paling towards night, Rosie went down and stood in the shallows and tried to steady herself against the ebb and flow of the water, tried to stay in one spot without having to shift her stance. She saw sand move away, then gush forward, felt the shape of it change under the balls of her feet. Grains of it, of land, came towards her, went again, became sea, went with the water.

Rosie wavered, like the water did; and just as it seemed never to waver, she sometimes felt absolutely sure – of her decisions, of things she'd left behind, of new ways offered her. And here at her feet, the water pulled in every direction at once, but it was always one thing: it was whole.

Rosie turned back towards the hill, towards hers and Cray's. She felt her feet subside slightly into the sand with each step. She paused at the bottom of the hill, tilted her face to the shacks and houses where evening lights were just beginning to glow.

The fig tree has grown gnarly over the years, since a young farmer first watered in its roots. But it fruits every summer, transforms from leafless winter sticks to a shady, heavy worker, wine-purple bulbs burgeoning. And if a hand does not reach up to gently test the darkening crop, or misses one in the picking, the fruit will drop to the ground.

Splitting open, a damaged fig reveals white maggoty seeds, oozing towards the soil. After the honeyeaters have had their share, the seeds end up in other backyards – under a washing line or hard up against a fence, and may or may not mature.

Here, in this rural garden, overlooking a sprawling, tired house, the greenest new leaves once again poke from leathery branches. An old woman hunches over small plants nearby, and a younger woman props herself against a marri's rough trunk. Tucked in the hollow arm of the marri is a boy's astronomy chart, rolled up safe and dry in a plastic bag.

If you stood beneath the marri tree you'd see it all. You'd see two men coming and going, stopping under the sky on clear nights. You'd see them working in silence in the plantation during the day. You'd see the years scudding across the sky as light, then dark, and all the shades in between.

Author's note

The events described in this book are a fictional reimagining of the Gracetown cliff collapse, which occurred at Huzza's Beach on 27 September 1996, and took the lives of nine people. While some of the events in the novel have some correlation to actual events, none of the characters in *The Break* are in any way based on the real people who were touched by this tragedy and are not intended to bear any resemblance to any living party.

To date, the Gracetown cliff collapse is Western Australia's worst natural disaster.

Acknowledgements

With each new book I embrace the word 'collaboration' with new gusto. There have been so many people who have contributed to this book, whether directly or indirectly.

The early drafts of *The Break* were written when I was a master's candidate at UWA in the mid-1990s. I thank Van Ikin for his gentle, expert guidance and kindness. Brenda Walker, Gail Jones and Dennis Haskell too offered support, advice and a writerly environment – thank you. I am also extremely grateful to the UWA Scholarships Office for its financial support over those two years.

The new-millennium drafts of this book were developed with the care and hard work of two wonderful editors: Amanda Curtin and Georgia Richter. Amanda did her best to logically position my jam doughnuts and Georgia swept up the sugar that was flung about in the process. They were unrelenting in their attention to detail and their determination to grasp the ungraspable. Thank you both so much.

Cate Sutherland deserves special thanks for her role in bringing this manuscript to the attention of Fremantle Press.

Thank you Ally Crimp for your wonderful design work, and Naama Amram, the proofreader's proofreader.

Fremantle Press staff have my enormous appreciation for their work in promoting me, selling my books, and managing everything else with such aplomb, including my impromptu visits to their office.

My special thanks to Susie Ormonde who answered all manner of questions (and some panicky text messages) about gardening in the south-west of Western Australia.

Thanks to my old boss George Williams for generously sharing his knowledge about newspaper reporting in the 1990s.

Stewart Dallas, thank you for answering every one of my questions about wind, swell and surfing, and for your constancy in our lives. Jerry and Pippa, you are the best fans a writing mum could have.

Mum and Dad, this one's for you. Thank you for everything.

First published 2014 by
FREMANTLE PRESS
25 Quarry Street, Fremantle 6160
(PO Box 158, North Fremantle 6159)
Western Australia
www.fremantlepress.com.au

Also available as an ebook.

Consultant editor Georgia Richter
Editor Amanda Curtin
Cover design Ally Crimp
Cover photograph Orien Harvey
Internal image from *The Zoology of the Voyage of HMS Erebus & Terror* by Sir James Clark Ross, courtesy of Western Australian Museum

A catalogue record for this book is available from the National Library of Australia

ISBN 9781922089632 (paperback)

Fremantle Press is supported by the Western Australian State Government through the Department of Cultural Industries, Tourism and Sport.

Publication of this title was assisted by the Commonwealth Government through Creative Australia, its arts funding and advisory body.

Fremantle Press respectfully acknowledges the Whadjuk people of the Noongar nation as the Traditional Owners and Custodians of the land where we work in Walyalup.

www.ingramcontent.com/pod-product-compliance
Lightning Source LLC
LaVergne TN
LVHW091128080826
845145LV00008B/2079
* 9 7 8 1 9 2 2 0 8 9 6 3 2 *